HUNTING: CARUSO MAFIA BOOK TWO

Nova Mason

ISBN: 8218182960
ISBN-13: 9798218182960

Cover Design: SelfPubBookCovers.com/PremiumRomance

WARNING:

"Hunting" is the second book in the Caruso Mafia series. It is a stand-alone Mafia Forced Proximity and Kidnapping Romance, complete with HEA and no cliffhangers.

Please note: this book is a mafia romance that contains mature content, graphic violence and may contain triggers. If such materials offend you, please do not read.

CHAPTER ONE

Seven Years Ago - Massimo

He's fucking drunk again.

Why am I not surprised? It's seven am on a Monday morning, why wouldn't my father be sleeping off his latest bender in a holding cell downtown? He has nothing better to do. He hasn't had a job in years. I pay his bills, buy his groceries, and even have a cleaning service at the house once a week. All his needs are taken care of by me.

I scrub my hand down my face. It does nothing to ease the tension in my body. I don't even know why I do it. Do I really think I can wipe away the stress that easy?

No. I do it because it's a habit to keep myself from taking out my aggression on an unsuspecting and undeserving bystander. Lucky for me. I happen to have a suspecting and deserving little bastard at my disposal this time.

The irritation I previously felt from the Police Captain's phone call fades away. The adrenaline of retribution now courses through my veins. I crack my neck and stretch my shoulders as I cross the room and join my latest victim once again.

Though, I shouldn't use the term victim. The prick deserves everything he has coming to him. "You're lucky Luca said not to kill you."

Luca is my best friend. He's also my boss. I report to him, and he reports to his Dad Ricco, the Underboss to the Caruso Mafia. As his firstborn male, Luca will inherit his position when Ricco retires.

"Personally I think you deserve it. You fucked us over Fred. You double crossed us." I hit him with a jab to the gut. He grunts in pain. "Weren't we good to you? We paid you handsomely, and all you had to do was keep our shipments off the manifests and the information to yourself. But you got greedy didn't you?"

He can't answer me. I broke his jaw before I was interrupted by my phone call. He can't look at me either. The punches to his face earlier have caused his eyes to swell shut. It will be a few days before he will be able to see clearly again.

His arms are tied up and stretched above his head. I hung him so his toes barely touched the floor. It's a classic torture method. Makes the person feel as though they have a smidgen of hope. Like a carrot dangled in their face.

"If I were you, I would get out of town. Run as far and as fast as you can." I pick up the metal baseball bat from my table of toys. I test its weight in my hands before I give it a swing. Fred lets out an ear piercing howl. "Whoops. Guess you won't be running. Maybe you can drive with your left leg." I put the bat bag on the table. I prefer to feel the blood of enemies on my hands. With that in mind, I work a combination of jabs, crosses, and hooks on Fred's immobile body.

He'll live, albeit painfully.

2

I wipe his blood off my knuckles with a towel, then give a nod to the two soldiers in the corner. They know my expectations for the clean-up, so I leave them to it while I hop into my Camaro.

It's time for me to pick up my father, Giuseppe D'Angelo. The cops know the drill. When they get a call for him, they are to pick him up, call me, and lock him up until I can get him. Nothing goes on his record. No reports are written up.

At one time my father was a soldier in the Caruso Mafia. He was part of the crew that padded the cops' pockets when we needed them to look the other way. That seems like a lifetime ago. In a sense it is. Nothing is the same as it was back then. Not me, my family, not even the Mafia.

When I was little, I had a two parent home. My father, the soldier, and my mother, Helen, a hairdresser. We weren't rich but we were happy. Or so I thought. Little did I know my mother was a lying, cheating, bitch. She had been sleeping around on my father while he had been working his ass off day and night, taking every job no matter how dirty or dangerous so we could have a better life. He knew she wasn't happy with our financial situation. To put it blunt, we were broke. Dirt ass poor. Living in a rundown trailer with a roof that leaked and a fridge that only worked half the time.

While my father had grown up middle class, my mother's family had lived beyond their poverty level means. Her father was a gambler. A bad one at that. He lost what little they had at the tracks. It got so bad he was taking cash he got from one loan shark to pay another.

At that time, my father and mother were recently married and expecting me. They had met in high school and it was love at first sight. Or so my father claims.

One night my father got a call for a job. A man was late on his payment. An example needed to be made. He couldn't do it. The man was his father-in-law. My dad went to the Don and begged him to reconsider. Told him he would take on his debts and work them off in exchange for leniency.

It was granted on the condition that my mother's parents leave the city and never come back. To this day, they haven't stepped foot in the city. I probably should feel bad for never knowing my grandparents. I don't.

My father ended up unable to afford our apartment and had to move us into the trailer park on the outskirts of town. It was only temporary. He promised my mom he would work the debts off quickly. The Don was a bastard. He kept adding interest, making it impossible for my family to crawl out of the hole they were in.

It wasn't until Dad's best friend Ricco had earned a favorable position with the Don's son, Bosco, after saving his life that things started to turn around. Bosco ensured my father was put under his command and paid him handsomely. Unfortunately it was too late for my mother. By then it had been years, and she had already left us.

Her betrayal wrecked my father. He was so in love with her, that he couldn't fathom how she was able to leave him. Especially after all he had done for her and her family.

Disloyal. That's what she is.

I despise disloyalty. Much like I despise cheating.

It's been years and my father still barely manages to be sober for more than a few hours. It's how he copes with the pain of her loss. With the loneliness. I want to hate him. I should hate him. He wasn't the only one who lost someone that day.

Actually I guess you could say I lost two someones.

In my teens I kept waiting for him to go back to the man he was. To put the bottle down and put me first. He didn't.

His actions forced me to grow up long before I should

have had to. Long before a child destined to be a made man in the family normally would. And that's saying something. All children in the family grow up early. It's how we survive. How we thrive.

If it weren't for Ricco, I would have been lost. More than likely, I would have been dead years ago. My blood splattered in a dark alley. I had so much anger in me, it made me dangerous, careless. Teachers wanted me to get medicated. Doctors wanted me in therapy. Ricco had other plans. He put me in a boxing ring and slapped some gloves on me.

Day after day, he forced me through the ropes. First letting me punch until I could no longer lift my arms, then later moving on to teaching me technique. Once I could take down men twice my size, he moved me on to weaponry. Pistols, revolvers, sniper rifle, knives, axes, bats, basically anything that could be fired, thrown, or swung he put in my hands and taught me to use it.

While I still check in on my father each week, I rarely spend more than a few hours with him. It's the only time in the week he stops bringing a bottle to his lips.

Ricco has been my father in his absence. His wife, Greta, my only mother figure.

God I love that woman. She has taken a wooden spoon to my ass more times than I can count. I deserved them.

She is an angel. A goddamn angel. If I ever marry, if I ever find a woman I can trust, I want her to be like Greta. Strong, resilient, and nurturing. As a grown man of twenty-one, she still dotes on me, and I love every moment of it. My cold dead heart soaks it up. Absorbs it like the black-hole it is.

I pull up to the front of the precinct and put my car in park. I don't turn it off. Leaving the keys in the ignition, I march through the front door. I won't be in there long.

Besides, no one will dare mess with my car, and not just because it's in front of a police station. I have built a reputation these last few years. My matte black Camaro is as synonymous with fear as the whisper of my name. Touching it will mean certain death for that individual.

Cops scurry out of my way. They won't exchange any pleasantries with me and that's fine by me. I don't need them as friends. They work for the family, and by extension, me. Every cop in this precinct does.

Rounding the corner, I find my father sitting slumped in a chair. Captain Richards stands beside him. I greet him with a nod of the head. "Good day Mr. D'Angelo. I'm sorry we interrupted your morning. As I said, I could have driven him home." His voice shakes as he speaks. God I love hearing the squeak of fear in his voice. It sends a rush of adrenaline down my spine.

I grab my father under his arm and get him to stand. He's losing weight again. Probably forgetting to eat in his drunken stupor. "Your offer is appreciated. Perhaps next time I will take you up on it." I swear his ego doubles in size. I turn my father towards the door. "Let's go dad."

Fuck he smells like whiskey and piss. I've come prepared. This isn't my first rodeo. I have a plastic covering already on the passenger seat. I won't risk the scent permeating into the leather.

I buckle my father in and before I get into the driver's seat, he's passed out. Figures. My temper rises a bit more as I pull out onto the street. I need a session in the ring. The serenity I found beating Fred is gone.

My father barely stirs as I get him out of my car and into his house. It's on the edge of the Caruso Family compound with a few acres of land and trees between it and Ricco and Greta's house. All higher ranking men of the family have a place at the compound. It's our home base of operations. The younger guys, like Luca and I, stay in the main house in our own apartments. Though my father is no longer an active member and never made it to the inner circle, his relationship with Ricco and my status in the family has granted him the special privilege of living here.

"I'm sorry son. You must be embarrassed by me." He slurs his words. It doesn't matter. I know them by heart. He says them every time I pick him up.

"Get some sleep dad." I give him a kiss on the temple. As angry as I am with him, and as disappointed as I am, I still love him.

He closes his eyes. "Your mother was right to leave me. I'm a pathetic excuse of a man."

Fuck. I don't want her to keep winning. The bitch hasn't been around in a long time. Her opinion no longer matters. It never should have.

"No." I jerk his shoulder so his eyes open again. "You are a good man. Lost. But a good man. Helen is the bitch. You saved her family. Took their debts and spared their lives. You gave her everything you could. Hell, you could have given her the Queen's crown jewels and the greedy bitch would have still wanted more."

"I love her." Emotions coat his words. I know he means them. Wish he didn't.

"Don't. She's been gone for years. You don't owe her anything more. Let her go dad."

"I can't." His eyes close again. Sleep pulling him under.

I pull the comforter up. "I know." I don't understand how he can still love her. I don't. At first I did. I did what all kids from broken homes do. Blamed myself. Took me a while to realize I was wrong. Nothing I could have done would have kept her from leaving.

Perhaps I am a naive idiot. I've never loved a woman. Not in the romantic sense. I've fucked woman. I've lusted over countless female forms. Never have I wanted a relationship. Never felt the pull on my heart and soul. Not sure I ever will. It would be simpler if I didn't.

My mind wanders to numerous possibilities of the future. What kind of woman could get me to fall in love with her? Is it possible? My heart has been dead for a while. If so, will it be a love at first sight situation? It was for both Ricco and my dad. One relationship is still going strong. The other failed miserable. Guess my odds are fifty-fifty.

I struggle to reign my mind in as I pull up to the main house. It's a massive mansion. Built like a fortress. It houses over a dozen apartments, as well as a war room, bunker, escape tunnel, and my personal favorite, the dungeon. It's where I learn the secrets of our enemies. I've perfected dozens of ways to extract information from even the most tight lipped individual.

Before I can get out of the car, Luca is rushing down the front steps. I wonder what set his ass on fire. He was called into a meeting with the Don Bosco early this morning. My best guess is the Don was grilling him on the debacle at the Port this weekend.

Fucking Fred.

His actions forced us into a fight with the Irish. We won. Of course. Didn't matter though, it sealed the Port Master's fate. He's not dead. Yet. I showed him leniency just as Luca asked. For now.

While I may not have agreed with Luca to let him live, I didn't go against him. I wouldn't. I respect him, and I trust him intrinsically. He's the calm to my storm. The cautious to my rash. The planner to my spontaneous. When someone betrays us I want to act. To punish. I don't give a damn the

8

reason. Luca thinks it through, sees the various angles and measures them to choose the most effective course of action.

My fist is effective.

Luca practically throws himself into the car. "Drive." He barks.

Something happened in that meeting. And it has nothing to do with the Port. I don't know how I know that. I just do. It's a gut feeling. And I always trust my gut.

The gates open for us without needing to stop. "Want to tell me about it?" I ask.

He huffs out a breath and drags a hand through his hair. It's cut similar to mine. Longer on top, short on the sides. Where his is straight, mine has a curl to it and several shades darker. I drag my eyes off the road and look at him. He's smiling. Like full on, crazy man smiling. My eyebrows raise. His facial expression making no sense after how he practically ran from the house.

"I'm getting married." He finally states. My breathing stops.

"What?" I slam my foot on the brake. The seatbelts catching us and slamming us back.

He turns to face me. The same goofy ass smile still on his face. "I'm going to be Don!" He exclaims proudly.

What!

My expression must give away my confusion. Thank god, because I can't get the words to form on my tongue to ask what the hell he is talking about.

"Bosco asked me to marry Milan and I accepted." Milan is Don Bosco's only child.

Now I have the words, "she's eight." Has he lost his damn mind?

Luca laughs and grabs my shoulder. "It's an arranged marriage. We won't be dating, we aren't expected to fall in love, and we won't marry until she turns eighteen. Besides, it will be worth it." His words are vague and I want to punch him. He knows what he's doing to me. He's riling me up. Fucker. "Milan is the Don's only daughter." He states matter-of-factly.

"I'm aware." The last of my patience is slipping away.

"He has no male heir."

Oh fuck! I know where this is going. Now I'm smiling too.

"I'm going to be Don." His grin gets even bigger.

I can't help but to repeat the sentiment. "You're going to be Don."

"And you my friend, are going to be my second." My jaw drops. Literally drops. Holy shit. "What do you say Massimo? You ready for all our dreams to come true?"

"Fuck yes!" Underboss. Luca is making me Underboss. The position was supposed to be his. Spots in the inner circle follow the bloodline unless there are extenuating circumstances. This is one. Bosco has no male heir. It's archaic but the mafia doesn't allow women to lead. Meaning Milan's husband will take up the mantle, as long as the Council approves the union. Which sounds like they already did, otherwise Luca wouldn't have had a contract to sign. "We need to fucking celebrate!" I shout as I throw my car back into gear.

Luca laughs. "Easy brother. We have a job to do first." Right. Shit. Work comes first. "Tonight we can party."

"You sure you're fiancé won't mind?" I joke. I've got ten year to give him shit, and I'm greatly looking forward to it.

"Fuck you!" He grits as he punches me in the arm. It hurts a bit. He's got a hell of a swing. Regardless, I deserved it. "I've got ten years to get my fill of pussy before I get hitched."

"You going to take your vows seriously?" I already know the answer, though I ask the question anyway. Luca is loyal as fuck. We both are. Not an ounce of deception in us. Luca would put a bullet in his mother's head before he broke a vow, and that's saying something. Luca worships Greta. Like I said, angel. Luca will honor his vows to Milan just as he honors his vows to the family. With every ounce of his being.

"Without question." His answer is just as I knew it would be.

"What if you fall in love?" It's a serious question. Our futures depend on him not fucking this up. Unlike me, Luca is open to the idea of marriage and a family. And ten years is a long time to play the field and avoid catching feelings.

He's quiet for a long moment. I know he's taking a moment to consider it. "I won't let anyone close."

"You sure about that? Ten years is a long time to be alone."

"Says the fucker who's never had a girlfriend." He laughs but it's not with humor. He knows I avoid relationships. I'm not against finding someone. At least I don't think I am. I'm just extremely picky. I need them to be loyal and trustworthy. If I doubt their intentions for even a moment I won't give them a chance. Luca takes a deep, audible breathe, and releases it slowly. "Being Don is what I always dreamed of and never thought I'd get. My father got lucky becoming Underboss and putting me in the position for this to happen. I won't screw this up."

"I've got your back brother." It goes without saying but I say it anyway.

Ten years.

We have ten years before we can take on our new positions. Ten years before Luca's nuts get trapped in a vice. Never to be free. I know my friend, he may not want to marry

Milan but he will treat her well and never bed another once the ring is on his finger.

I wonder what fate awaits me in that department.

I shake my head in the hopes of shaking the thoughts away. It's time to get to work. Then tonight, we celebrate, and get him laid.

He's only got ten years to satisfy him for a lifetime.

CHAPTER TWO

Present Day - Livianna

I pull the collar of my coat up a bit higher as I cross the campus to the coffee shop. My friend Ashley asked me to meet her there. She is going to regale me with the latest gossip around campus, and most certainly the latest tale of her boyfriend's screw ups. It's going to be a long hour. I don't mind playing the dutiful friend. She's the only one I am close to at the moment and as much as I could care less about gossip and wish she would dump the dumb prick she's dating, I put up with it so I don't alienate yet another person in my life.

I don't mean to. I don't do it on purpose. At least not consciously. My father has a dangerous job. One with a lot of secrecy. Secrets that I shouldn't know. Yet many I had a hand in him learning. With my father's position, I can't risk people getting too close. Consequently, I end up seeming like a bitch. Maybe after his upcoming promotion I can relax. He'll be in a stable position, one that takes him off the streets. Hopefully one I won't need to partake in anymore. Which means no more secrets. No more stress. No more late night gallivants around town doing shady shit.

It's all for a good cause, I remind myself. Dad needed the help. I needed him off the streets and out of danger. And we needed the money.

As a kid, I took for granted the amenities and luxuries we had. We were by no means rich. We were comfortable. More importantly, we were happy. Still are. Just a little less.

Things changed when my mother got sick. Cancer. She fought like the warrior she was. We got eight months longer than the doctor's predicted with her. Even without hair, body frail, and intense pain radiating throughout her entirety, she never stopped smiling. Or laughing. I miss her laugh. Dad does too. He took a lot of time off when she got sick. Caused us to have to sell our house and most of our worldly possessions. I didn't care. Neither did he. Each item we sold was another handful of minutes we got to stay by mom's side.

It's been five years. I still miss her every day. So does dad.

It gets better. The pain isn't as sharp. Just a dull ache. One I can live with. It means I remember her.

Dad's doing better too. He took a bit of time off after the funeral before getting back to work. His boss was nice and continued to pay him. Even paid for mom's funeral and hospital expenses. He said if he had known he would have helped sooner. It's the reason why I help my dad. Loyalty. Dad wants to repay his boss for his kindness. I want to continue to see my dad living and not succumbing to darkness that threatens his heart without mom around to bring him back to the light. He was a wreck after mom died. He needed a passion. He found it in his job. Just needed a bit of a push. One I was happy to give.

Now he's thriving at work and the boss has taken notice. I'm proud of him. Even if it means I spend more nights helping him than studying, even if my help means endangering myself and pushing me far beyond my comfort zones.

I let out a deep sigh as I reach the shop and open the door. The smell of roasted coffee beans seeps into my lungs. Damn do I love the smell. Even if I hate the taste. I can tolerate espresso but only if it is drowned in milk and caramel. Ashley makes fun of me. Tells me it can't count as coffee when it's prepared like that. She's right. It's a latte, or a macchiato. Depends on my mood.

A quick scan of the room has my feet leading me over to a table in the back. Ashley is sitting hunched over her phone. Her still full coffee untouched beside her. Damn. That means there's big drama going on between her and her man.

Well, not man. That's being too nice. He's a boy in a twenty year old's body.

I detest drama. If a relationship causes this much heartache and anxiety, why stay in it? It's a question I have asked Ashley several times and I won't be asking again. Her answer never changes. She says it's because she loves him. Why does loving someone mean you sacrifice your happiness for theirs? Hell, I'm not even sure she is happy. They spend all their time fighting, arguing, ignoring, and stalking each other. Their actions are so chaotic and confusing. Not to mention they have only been dating for two months. My god, do they even know each other enough to say they love one another?

What's worse is, they aren't alone in their idiotic thinking. So many students and just people in general claim to love the person they are with. Yet, too easily they dump them and move onto the next. I don't understand. Maybe it's because I can't share parts of my life with anyone so I don't get close enough to risk falling in love. At least not in the romantic sense. I love my parents, I love Ashley like a sister. But to love a man? Nope. Never done it. Never felt it.

The thought saddens me and has me pausing before I reach the table. Do I want love? Is that why I feel this sense of longing. I thought it was lack of fulfillment. Lack of moving forward. I go to classes, and study, but it feels like I'm waiting for the next step in life. I thought that would be graduating in a few months and getting a job, starting a career.

Maybe it's more than that.

Ashley finally looks up and sees me. She smiles brightly. I push the thoughts to the back of my mind where they will remain locked away for the next hour or so.

Immediately Ashley goes into a rant about her boyfriend. "He's such an asshole. I swear, he does shit just to piss me off so we can have make-up sex."

Her statement catches me off guard and I struggle to keep my drink from expelling out my nostrils. "What?"

"You know. That rough and angry kind of sex. The push you up against the wall, rip your clothes off, smack your ass kind." She says it with no hesitation or shame. Her words are smooth in delivery. Like talking about the weather. Meanwhile I'm struggling to keep my composure and the blush from taking over my face.

I am aware of what sex is. I even know what she meant when she said make-up sex. I'm not a Nun. Well, not completely. I've kissed a few guys, messed around with some light touching. Nothing with the clothes off. I can't tell Ashley that. Logically I know I can. I don't think she would judge me. The opposite really. I think she would make it her personal mission to get me laid.

Part of me wants to let her. I want to know what it feels like to experience that level of intimacy with someone. Problem is, I don't want it with a stranger. I don't want it with a random hook-up, or some man child at school. I'm not waiting for marriage per-say or even love. I want a connection. I want to feel like more than a notch on the guy's bed post.

I also want to avoid having my own horror story. In high school my friend at the time, Jasmine, lost her virginity in the back of some guy's rusty truck in the high school parking lot after a football game. She said he reeked of body odor and dripped sweat on her for the two thrusts he got in before he was done. She didn't even get off and he dropped her off at her house afterwards without a kiss or even a good-bye.

Another girl I know waited until freshman year at college. She had been dating a guy for a few months before he pressured her into having sex at a frat party. He had been feeding her drinks all night so she wouldn't say no. She didn't. She should have. She said it hurt and he stuck his dick in the wrong hole first, so she lost two virginities that night. He broke up with her a week later. Calling her a frigid bitch.

Yeah. I'm good with keeping this my secret and waiting until I'm ready. Even if it means I reach thirty with my hymen intact.

"Right." I say. I'm at a loss for what else to add to that portion of the conversation, so I decided to lead it back to the problem. "So, what did he do?"

"He started following that slut Abby on social media." Ah, Abby. A female who shares several classes with Ashley's boyfriend. I am very familiar with her. Not personally of course. Never seen nor met her.

Ashley looks at me like she expects me to be outraged. I suppose that is the reaction that I should give. I don't. The conversation usually goes faster for me if I don't antagonize her into sharing every minute detail, repeatedly. She does enough of it without prompting.

"He liked her profile picture. She's wearing a bikini. Like come on. Have some class." I want to laugh. My tongue is pressed firmly between my teeth to stop me. Ashley has a ton of bikini photos online. They just aren't her profile picture.

Instead of staying quiet, I go for sarcastic. "How dare she?"

"Right! I mean damn. Attention whore much?" Yep, sarcasm went right over Ashley's head. It usually does. Doesn't matter. I keep listening and adding minimally to the conversation. It's what she needs. Besides, her venting gives me time to observe the people around the room. It's a hobby of mine. Actually more of a passion.

I've always been good at reading people. Reading their emotions, their expectations, their motivations, and even next moves. My dad says I am a human hacker. I'm told I should treat it like a gift. Use it to my advantage. I do. And I hate myself for it. It's become like second nature, and has caused some awkward social interactions on my part.

In recent months, I've been working to build on my skills, as well as develop the skill to filter my actions and words. I need to hone them. Too many times I end up divulging someone else's secrets too soon. Like a woman's pregnancy to her husband at the grocery store. It wasn't his baby. He was infertile. Or the one time I got a teen arrested for stealing. Turns out it was baby formula for his hungry little sister. He was wrong to steal but I felt guilty as hell for not finding out why and helping him before the cops got involved. Luckily I was able to get the store to forget the matter, even gave the kid a part time job. I also bought enough formula for the sister to last her until kindergarten. Not that she will be using it that long.

Filtering myself makes me feel like an impostor. My personality is no longer my own. My actions no longer instinctual. Each word, each step is carefully calculated so as to not offend or disgrace anyone else. Even my best friend is not safe from the game I have been forced to play within my head. I don't want to lose her or anyone else from my life. It's selfish. I suck at making friends. Suck more at keeping them. So far Ashley doesn't appear to be going anywhere. I intend to keep it that way.

Guilt eats at me as I realize I have tuned out her venting session completely. "Thanks for listening." She says. Her hand covers mine before she leans over and hugs me. "You're such a good friend." I smile into her hair as I reciprocate the hug.

Twenty minutes later and an overwhelming amount of campus gossip, she leaves feeling lighter and thanking me again for always being there for her. As I watch her leave, I feel my phone buzzing in my pocket.

No. Not tonight.

I haven't looked at my phone, but I know who it is. My dad.

My insides are turning and I have the desire to vomit. There is only one reason he would be calling me today. He needs help with a job. A mission. Damn.

I take a fortifying breathe before answering the phone.

I can't wait until I am free. Until I can end this charade and find the real me again. Minus the secrets.

I love my dad. I will do anything for him. He's all the family I have after mom died.

Dad makes the call short and sweet. He needs help on a job. Will give me details when I get to the house.

Looks like I'm going out tonight. Double damn.

I get to my father's house just after dinner. He wanted to eat together. I couldn't stomach it. Not with the nerves eating away at my belly. I should be used to it. I'm not.

Dad's in the kitchen when I get to the house. He greets me with a hug and a kiss on the cheek. "Thank you for coming sweetheart. This should be the last time. I can feel it. This is the one we've been searching for."

"You sure dad?" I trust him. He doesn't send me in without doing his due diligence.

He nods. "Yes. It's him. Just need the confession."

"Okay dad." I pause to steady myself. "Where am I going?"

The bar the target is expected at is a hip new bar in downtown. Tons of college students should be in attendance. Dad goes over the plan. It's similar to all the others. Get in, get close, get them out. We go over the finer details of the location, the car, the back-up plans, all of it.

"What information are we looking for? What is it he's suspected of doing?" I ask.

Dad looks like he won't answer me. But he knows the rules. I won't go if I don't know the facts. Even if they make my blood boil with rage or my stomach curdle with fear.

Tonight it is fear. That man is suspected of betraying the family. He's working with another one. One who deals in far shadier shit than we do. Human trafficking.

Shit. Shit. Shit. That's the real deal. And dad's right. This is the big fish he's been waiting for. If we get a confession out of him, the promotion is Dad's. With all that's on the line, I'm almost more excited to get this creep off the streets. Dad can do what he wants with him and I will sleep like a baby tonight.

With the details settled, I need to work on calming my nerves, so I change the subject to dad's promotion and the perks it will come with.

Dad's eyes light up instantly. "Boss says the new job will have me living on site. You can come with me. I've already gotten it approved."

"That's great dad. But I have my own place." He looks momentarily disheartened before the look vanishes. I tried to remind him softly. He doesn't like that I rent a one bedroom off campus.

"I know. And I'm proud as hell of you." His smile is genuine.

"Maybe we can set me up with a room so that I can visit often." I offer.

The smile grows wider again. "Absolutely."

"So tell me about the new job." I don't need to fain interest. I am genuinely curious.

"Boss says that changes are coming. Big changes. All for the better. They want to make sure we are solid. Going to be more training. Specific to what we've been doing. Well me. The information gathering." I don't interrupt or correct my father. While yes he does gather a lot of information once he has a bat or blade in his hand, it is my initial interaction that gets them talking first. You can teach it, to a degree. I've been trying for years to teach dad. Best I could do is point out markers that are typical indicators of lying. If he learned anything, I'm glad it was that.

The more dad talks about the jump, the more I agree that the position sounds perfect for him. Dad has a soft spot for the young soldiers. Always has.

The new job means less risk for him and free housing. He will finally be able to get out of this crappy trailer that's been falling apart since before we moved in when I was a teen. I'm thankful for this house though. For as cramped and as shitty as it was, it kept us warm and dry. In a weird way I'll miss it while simultaneously be excited to never see it again.

My father wasn't a perfect dad in my youth, but he tried. Damn did he try. Worked himself to the bone trying to move up from lowly soldier even before mom passed. He'd be the first to admit he isn't book smart. Didn't even graduate high school. I think he had potential. Potential no one else saw and therefore couldn't cultivate. Once I noticed, I did.

I can't take all the credit for the upward momentum in his career. He puts in the work. Does the grunt work and the dirty jobs. No one can ever know, but he's been my personal project. I've spent years tending to my father in a way that hasn't emasculated him in front of others.

I feel kind of like a mad scientist at times. I push him in the direction I want him to go and line up the tools he'll need along that way. It's the opposite of the saying you can lead a horse to water but you can't make them drink. Screw that. If you know what you're doing you sure as hell can. I lead my father to water and he drinks, then he fills up a canteen with more for later.

Though I will admit I may have pushed him too far. He's taken my extremes and grown them. Now I'm wrapped up in his business too. A business I have no place being in. But I love my dad and for that I'll do anything he asks of me. Even if there is ample risk.

I've let my mind wander too far. He's stopped talking. Waiting for me to reply or at least acknowledge what he has said. I just smile and nod. It's appears to placate him and he goes back to talking as though I am listening intently.

Tonight I'll go out one more time. One final big fish to secure dad's new position in the mafia. One more. I can do that. Then I can go back to my boring simple life.

A short time later, I'm excusing myself to go to my old room. I keep my clothes here that I use for these missions. It's just easier to get ready here after dad and I go over the finer points of the mission. As I close my bedroom door. I turn around and lean against it and give myself a minute.

My stomach is in knots again. Something about tonight feels different. I'm just not sure what. It's making me second guess the risk of going after this target. It's hitting closer to home than I am comfortable with. The guy is also presumed to be involved in selling girls. One wrong move tonight and I could be his next victim. Kidnapped, bought, sold, and shipped off to some far corner of the world to be a toy for some sick fuck.

Dad had assured me everything would be fine. Just like always. He promises he's got my back.

I take a deep breath before pulling myself away from the door to get ready. Once dressed, I check and double check that I have my pepper spray, knife and gun hidden on me. Then I look into the mirror and go through the last piece of my routine.

The pep talk.

Ending it with a reminder. If caught, don't talk. Never reveal who you work for. Don't trust anyone you don't know. Even if they show documents. They can be spoofed.

One more mission. One more night. I've got this. What could go wrong?

CHAPTER THREE

Livianna

I don't have this.

The man is an utter creep. He's not even drunk and he's being grabby. He makes my skin crawl. I'm ready to call the mission off and leave. The only reason I don't is because this is too important. I need to get this guy's trust. At least enough for him to invite me to his place, or a hotel. I'm not picky on details. We'll never make it there anyway. Once outside this bar, dad will take over and I can head back to my apartment.

I want this bastard off the streets. He hasn't confessed but I know he runs girls. It's a hunch. A good one. Based on several indicators I've read off of him. His biggest tell is the way he looks like he sees dollar signs every time he looks at a woman. The younger they are, the more he stares.

It is taking everything in me not to pull out my knife and stab him. Over and over again.

Then again. And again.

When this guy isn't looking at other women, his eyes are darting all around the room. He seems on edge. Barely keeping up with conversation. Which is fine. I'm spewing bullshit anyway. Seems I don't want to be here anymore than him. I only have his attention when he is staring down my dress or attempting to slide his hand up it.

Suddenly an arm is on mine and squeezing. Not hard enough to hurt, but hard enough to know the guy wants my attention. Demanding it really.

"There you are sweetheart." Says a deep voice in my ear. It sends a shiver down my back and has me clenching my thighs together. Hands down sexiest voice I have ever heard and I haven't even seen the face or body it goes with.

But putting your hands on me. Oh hell no.

Guys are constantly touching without an invite. It's one thing if they are my target. Strangers. Nope. No way. They need to learn a lesson.

Without pause, I spin around and rip my arm from his grasp in the process. Behind me, I hear my target scamper off. Damn it. I almost had him.

"I am not your sweetheart." I growl at the stranger. He's handsome. A solid eleven out of ten. Big, hard muscles force his shirt to stretch across his chest and biceps. It takes a lot of self-control to keep from drooling. I may be a virgin, but I deeply appreciate the male form. Especially ones with this amount of muscle. His face is gorgeous too. It should be a sin to look this good.

"No, but you could be." His lips curl into a tentative smile as he speaks. I can't tell if he's holding back the real smile to downplay his interest, or if he's doing it on purpose to play coy about flirting. Damn. More than ever I wish I had experience in flirting with hot guys. It's easy when the guy isn't attractive. Hot guys tend to know they are hot and it's a confidence killer to someone like me who is on the curvier side and never spent much time with a guy.

"Excuse me?" I'm trying to be polite, but he fucked up my mission and I am not in the mood for flirty banter.

"How much?" He asks as he leans against the bar. His elbow resting on the hard wood.

My eyebrows furrow in confusion. "What?"

"There's no way you were actually interested in that guy. Which means he must have paid you." Fuck this guy. I go to walk around him but he stops me. "We're not done talking."

"I am."

"We'll see about that."

I feel cold metal against my hip. "Let's go out back." A gun. I'm not afraid. Well, I am. But only a little. I know I'm not completely helpless. I've trained for this and I might be able to disarm him even with him being larger and stronger than me. I've practiced hundreds of times, dozens of scenarios and gotten good. In theory. I haven't yet had a real life experience to utilize my knowledge and skills. He's significantly larger than me and his muscles don't look like they are for show. I'll need to be smart when I make my move. Maximum pain with minimal effort and then a quick escape.

Doing as he says, I grab my coat off the chair. Being careful to keep my purse hidden beneath it. My knife is strapped to my thigh, my gun is in my purse. I won't be able to retrieve it without alerting him to what I'm doing, so I wait.

I let him take me to the alley. Once outside I grip his wrist in one hand and the gun in the other and give a quick twist while bringing my knee to his nuts. He's a big guy so I needed to multi-task my attacks in order to be effective. It worked. I now have the gun. I flick off the safety. Hoping since he still had it on, it means he wasn't planning to kill me, just scare me.

I increase the space between us and aim it at his chest.

"Easy sweetheart. Just need to talk." He says through pained breathes. He's still hunched over a bit. Good.

"So talk." I reply. I'm not sure what he wants with me. If it's an apology for calling me a hooker he would have done it inside.

"Afraid it's not that simple. You've been seen around town with a lot of different men the last few nights."

Shit. He's been following me. Why? "How is that your concern?"

"Typically it wouldn't be. I don't judge people's sex lives. You want to be a slut and spread your legs for everyone be my guest."

I am far from a slut. My lady bits have never seen action. Though I won't admit that to him. It's not his fucking business. "I am not a slut! I went out for drinks with them. I didn't sleep with them." Jesus.

His breathing has evened out and he's back to standing tall. "You left the bar with all of them and got into a car together."

"Putting aside the obvious stalking you've been doing which we'll come back to, yes I left with many of them, not all, some I left in their car, others we went inside and had a night cap and I left."

"That's it?" His eyes say that he doesn't believe. I don't give a shit if he does. I don't know him, and I certainly don't owe him anything.

"That's all I'm telling you." I retort. Stepping another few steps backwards. I'm almost to the end of the alley. Once I am, I plan on making a run for my father's location.

"Then why don't you tell me why six out of the last ten guys you've been seen leaving a bar with were found dead within days if not hours of last being seen with you?"

"I..." I'm not sure how to explain it. I can't tell him about my father's mafia involvement. This man could be mafia too for all I know. And if he is, the likelihood that he works for the same family as my father is minimal at best. I'm saved from lying when the man continues talking as though I hadn't tried to explain.

"Let me finish." I wait. He quirks the corner of his mouth up again. "And the other four have obviously had the shit kicked out of them but refused to talk."

I remain quiet. Fuck! Dad hasn't been as discreet as we thought. Though I'm not sure why this guy cares. Unless he's from one of the families. Shit. Russian maybe? He seems like a big asshole. Though he doesn't have a hint of an accent. Not that that is a requirement. It's more of an observation I have made.

We continue to argue for a few minutes. Him wanting me to explain the men's injuries and disappearances, and me asking for information about himself. I'm trying to read his body language but it's oddly statuesque. Like he doesn't have emotions. It makes it impossible to read him.

We aren't getting anywhere and I can't, and won't, reveal my true purpose with meeting with all of those men. I don't know who this man works for. I'm still leaning towards the Russians, or a new gang looking to gain some territory. Obviously not Italian.

Suddenly I feel a prick on my neck. I spin on my heel. My body going lax involuntarily as I do so. Did I spin too fast? Did I make myself light headed?

A pair of arms wraps around my waist to hold me up. My body feels light but my muscles are responding as though they are held down with lead weights. The gun in my hand slips through my fingers. I barely hear it clatter to the ground. My ears are ringing. My vision blurring. I try to scream for my dad but no sound comes from my throat.

No, no, no. This can't be happening.

"Easy sweetheart. Go to sleep. We'll see each other again soon." Whispers the gorgeous stranger.

Within moments, blackness engulfs me.

CHAPTER FOUR

Massimo

"Give it a second." I say with a laugh to Luca as we stand dressed in our Sunday best at the altar of church. It's his wedding day. It's three years earlier than he thought. It turns out Bosco had another daughter. One he didn't know existed until recently. With her discovery, the contract Luca had with Milan became null and void. Elena, is Bosco's firstborn, so the role of marrying Luca has fallen to her.

Not that it is a hardship. Luca fell in love with Elena the moment she held a gun to his head and kicked him in the nuts. Weird fucker.

He fell fast and hard. She was a bit slower to come around. She came to the city for two purposes. To get her mom a kidney. And to cross off each name on her list. Each one had wronged her or her family in some way.

Turns out, Elena's mom, Violet, was Bosco's high school sweetheart. They had married in secret at eighteen and got pregnant. Only Bosco never knew about the baby. His Uncle Santo had run Violet out of the city and sent a team of hit-men after them. He then told Bosco that she died in a car accident.

With the hit-men after Violet and Elena, they were forced to always be on the move. Never staying to plant roots anywhere.

This past week, Elena crossed the last name off her list. She has no reason to run anymore. Though that fact hasn't stopped Luca from panicking.

Like now, Luca's eyes are locked on his soon to be father-in-law's lone figure at the end of the aisle. His bride is late. I don't think Elena will run. In fact, I know she won't. I think she is screwing with him. Getting him worked up for no reason.

Looking around the crowded church, I take a moment to appreciate the life we have built. The friends we have made. The loyalty we have gained. It wasn't easy, even with Luca's dad's position. Honestly, Ricco being Underboss probably made things harder. We couldn't get away with shit. All eyes were on us. We had to be better.

I get lost in the memories for a moment before I physically shake my head in an effort to clear up my thoughts. I should be focused on the present. On Luca and the security of his new bride. I should be buzzing with the excitement of my new position. Underboss. In no time at all, it will be mine.

Mine.

It's a word that has popped into my head a few times in recent days. So little has been solely mine in life. My pain is also my father's. My work is also Luca's. My loyalty is also the family's. What if anything is mine? My car is mine I guess.

Not sure how my mind goes from my car to the woman in the basement of the compound. She's been there for two days and refuses to speak a word since waking up.

I'm out of my depth with her. I am an enforcer, an information gatherer. It's my main purpose within the family, regardless of my position. It's what I was born to do. No one is immune to my techniques. I have had years of practice getting even the most tight lipped man to talk. Sometimes those techniques get a little bloody. Few can stomach being in the room with me when I have a man in my chair or on my table.

I don't blame them. In another life. If I was another man. Or wasn't part of the family, I too might find it repulsive and sickening.

Problem I'm running into is, I'm not dealing with a man.

I've never tortured a woman and I don't plan on starting now. Even if she does work for the enemy. I've kept my punishments minimal so far. I don't want to cause her physical trauma, so I have stayed with psychological, and even those methods are tame. For now. The day is rapidly approaching when I'll need to either up the ante or switch to physical methods.

Luca has sensed my hesitation with the woman. Though we are not blood brothers, we were raised with the same values. Woman and children are off limits. Elena, my friend's bride-to-be does not possess the same reservations.

Elena's high strung conviction takes some getting used to. Which is weird because I'm usually like that as well. Just not when it comes to this woman apparently. She has gotten under my skin. That has never happened before. I'm in unchartered territory and I don't like it. I hate it. I can't trust my gut, and I've always been able to do that. My gut is torn. It's loyal to the family and wants to extract the secrets she holds, while another part of me wants to pull her from the dungeon, drag her to my bed and make her mine. I've even found myself hoping this is all a misunderstanding and that the next time I go down to see her she will explain how everything was just some strange coincidence and she has horrible taste in men.

When Luca and I told Elena about our guest in the basement, she instantly volunteered to be the one to interrogate her. And by interrogate, she meant torture. Blood, gore, violence, screams, and pain that would make a normal, or rather, an average woman squeamish. Not Elena. She's like us. Gets an adrenaline rush. And she has no qualms with doing it to a woman.

As much as I want answers, I can't send Elena down. Not yet. Maybe I'm delusional. Maybe I'm thinking with my cock, but I don't want to hurt her. I want to believe that somehow she is innocent in all of this and won't illicit a war when we release her.

Finally Elena appears at the end of the aisle. Thank fuck! I don't have time to go hunting for her again. I give Luca's shoulder a squeeze then step back to my assigned position. Behind me Luca's brother Val chuckles. Elena was never going to run. She's too infatuated with Luca. Their marriage may be written in a contract, but the love the two share isn't something that you can put into words on paper. Hell, not even their marriage license will be adequate enough to encompass their feelings. If ever I believed in soul-mates it would be them.

Luca needed someone strong to stand at his side. As boss there will be countless threats to him and his family. A typical housewife wouldn't be able to handle his late nights, the calls at three in the morning, or the unexplained blood on his clothes.

When Elena first arrived I feared she might actually be too much for Luca. Hell, she's had more blood on her hands these few weeks than him. Then again, she has been invaluable in helping us extricate our rats. Blood spilling was necessary. So far we have exterminated seven. We are missing one. That's where the woman in the basement comes in. From the intelligence we have gathered, she has had contact with a lot of bad man on our list. Damn near all. A few of which have ended up in our basement after one of our enforcers tracked them down and brought them in for questioning.

There is something we are missing. A piece to this puzzle that only she can unlock. If only she would talk. She's stubborn. Or smart. Both I think. She doesn't think she should trust us. If she is innocent she has nothing to fear. I've told her as much. I can see the distrust in her eyes. Someone has taught her well. Trust no one.

Part of me hopes she is being coerced into seeking these men out. If she's being threatened I can help her. I just need her to fucking talk.

"Break her heart and I will destroy you." Threatens Bosco.

Luca smiles in return. "Never. Her heart is safe with me."

"And yours with me." Replies Elena.

Gag.

Luca pulls Elena in close and plants a kiss far too inappropriate for a church on her lips. "Nope." I say with a shake of my head. "Nope, none of that. You need to say I do first." I love my best friend and am happy for him, but if we have to wait until he gets his fill of Elena we will be here all damn night. And I have shit to do. I need to see my woman.

My woman?

Nope.

The woman.

"Pussy blocker." Quips Elena. Her brash words force me

to laugh, as do many in the church pews. I watch and smile with pride as my friend marries the love of his life. Afterwards, me, and the rest of the guests, follow them to the reception back at the compound.

I do my best to keep my head on straight. To not think of the woman in the basement. I fail miserably. Even Val and Milan's silly antics and forcing of the DJ to play the "Chicken Dance" in a room full of dark and dangerous mafia men doesn't keep my attention for long.

The moment Luca and Elena make their escape to their private quarters, I head downstairs.

CHAPTER FIVE

Livianna

It's freezing in the basement. When I woke up I was locked in a cell. My dress gone. It's been two days. I think. Time is hard to judge with no clock or windows to use as reference. My guess is based on the meal delivery times.

Meals. I guess that's what you call them. They are no more than a piece of toast and a bottle of water three times a day. I eat very little and drink even less. I'm fearful of what poisons await me in them. Seeing as they used a drug to knock me out and get me here, I can only guess that they have no qualms with using other chemicals either.

My captor has been down to visit me several times. Staying long hours. He hasn't touched me. At least not that I am aware of. He hasn't come into my cell since I woke up and when I did, I felt no pain or discomfort in or on my body. Not even between my legs which had been my first panic when I opened my eyes and realized I was in only my bra and undies on a thin, dirty mattress on the floor of a dark room with bars as three of the walls.

I was a virgin when I went to the bar that night, and I strongly feel I still am. I'm certain I would feel it if that was not the case.

Still. I cannot trust my captor or his men. I know not where I am. I want to ask. Many times I have opened my mouth to speak. I just can't bring myself to do it. Any or all words out of his mouth could be a lie. I have no reason to trust him.

Should I trust him?

There is pain in his eyes each time I refuse to answer him. It disappears quickly. It makes me wonder how much patience for me he has left. Aside from the lack of clothes and blankets that make it nearly unbearably cold, the small portions of food, and the humiliating bucket in the corner that is meant as my toilet, the only other things they have done is keep me awake.

The whole time!

I get why they are doing it. It's to break me. Lack of sleep is a torture my father has spoken of frequently. Lack of sleep messes with your mind. I'm holding strong so far. I think. I mean, at least outwardly. I haven't opened my mouth to spew any secrets. Or any words at all. My cheeks have felt the pain. I have bitten them so much to keep my jaw from opening that I fear I may tear through my cheeks.

I've drifted off a few times, my body not giving me any choice. Each time I am woken with either blasting music or cold water being splashed on me after far too short a time to feel rested. My guess is those nap have been no longer than ten to twenty minutes. Currently I am curled in the far corner of my cell with the mattress propped up in front of me. I have no blanket to ward of the cold, or the creepy stares of the guards. I've had to make do with what I have. Which is my bucket-o-toilet and this mattress.

Not all of the guards are bad. Some look at me with pity, some ignore me, one in particular leers at me as though he is waiting for the opportunity to sneak into my cell and do god knows what to me. Thankfully he is not on shift right now. The one that ignores me is.

I hear a door opening somewhere in the distance. Great. I was nearly asleep. Again. Please don't be the creepy guard. I'm too tired. I don't feel comfortable trying to get even a moment of sleep with him watching.

The clicking of dress shoes on the cement floor draws my eyes up. My eyes connect with my handsome captor. I can't help my eyes from wandering up and down him. He has always worn suits. Not like this though. This one is formal wear. I wonder where he has been.

"Hey sweetheart! Did you get a good nap?"

Fucker. I hate that my heart flutters at the nickname. It's nearly more torturous than anything else he has done. I have had one boyfriend in my life and he was a jerk. We dated for six months my freshman year of college. He didn't like that I wanted to wait to have sex with him. He kept trying to pressure me into doing it. I finally had enough and broke up with him.

I was heartbroken and hoping it would be temporary and he would realize that he loved me and would wait until I was ready and patch things up with me. It wasn't temporary and I never want to see the bastard again. I found out that not only did he sleep with someone else the night I broke up with him, but he had been sleeping with a long string of girls while we were together.

The door to my cell opens and rips me from my thoughts. I press further into the wall. Yeah. Like that will help. It's not like it will open up and swallow me up. It's useless. Still my body tries. I pull the mattress closer, keeping a white knuckled grip on it.

It's no use. The man crosses the room quickly and rips it away from me. Not only that, but he tosses it out of the cell. "No!" The word leaps from my mouth before I can stop it.

"She talks."

Shit. I don't say another word. My cheeks are clenched in my teeth. I can taste my own blood from the force I use. I don't relent.

"Don't be shy." He takes a step closer again. I know it's foolish but I turn my head and allow my hair to create a veil between us. "Don't be like that." His fingers grasp my chin and turn my head towards him. I keep my eyes down. His voice is soft. Almost caring. "I haven't hurt you." My eyes fly up to his. Lies. "Not physically anyway." I squint my eyes and furrow my brow at his statement.

While he may not have kicked, punched, or drawn blood, I wouldn't say my punishment hasn't been physical. My body has been wracked with shivers since I woke up. The several buckets of water they have tossed on me has only made it worse. I'm surprised my teeth haven't shattered from their constantly clashing while my body instinctually tries to warm itself up.

Looking into his eyes I can see he is waiting for me to answer. Still I don't speak.

He laughs and releases my chin. "Not yet anyway. Truth is. That's up to you." He grabs me roughly by the arm and yanks me to my feet.

With a firm grip, he pulls me out of my cell and down the wide hallway. He brings me into a new room. There is a lone chair under a single bright light-bulb in one half of the room, and what looks like a doctor's examination table centered in the other half. The back wall is cluttered with what can only be described as a wall of horrors. Chains, knives, guns, belts, whips, spikes, a few different axes, rope, and various other items.

I gulp. Hard. My mouth is dry and the little spit I have doesn't want to go down my throat. My captor pulls me towards the chair and pushes me into it. He isn't as rough as I imagine he could be. The pain is internal. A soul eating pain. There is a strong chance that I will not leave this room. How long will I last? Will he make my death quick if I do not answer? Should I try to answer? Is my loyalty to the family my dad pledged us to worth my death?

Would anyone other than my father miss me? Fuck. Why did I have to be such a hermit? Why didn't I live more while I could?

Straps tighten around my wrist and ankles. I test them. They touch my skin yet don't bite into my flesh. That will come later. My imagination conjures up a thousand horrors. Shit. I usually love my imaginative mind. Not now. Not here in this room. Those bloody fucked up visions could come to life. This room has the tools to do it. And I sensed the danger that lurks in my captor since the moment his hand first touched me.

Foolishly I had also found safety in his touch. It was startling, and I didn't like that he did it with my back to him, or even the circumstances in which it happened. Yet, my mind has wondered a hundred times what it would have been like to have met him under different circumstances. What it would have been like to have him hold me and call me "sweetheart" with the conviction my heart wants to believe he says it with.

"I am giving you one more chance sweetheart." Damn that name. "I am going to ask you some questions, and I need you to answer them. Truthfully." He circles me so he is to my back and I hear the clanking of unknown metal objects behind me.

Panic threatens to overwhelm me. Stay strong Livianna, I tell myself.

Hands empty, he comes around to my front. "I don't want to hurt you." His voice is softer than before. Emotions swirl in his eyes. I want to believe him. Damn, do I want to believe him. "How about I start out with something simple."

He pauses. His eyes locked with mine.

"What is your name?" I hesitate. He sighs loudly. His head hanging. Maybe he isn't such a bad guy after all. Maybe he won't hurt me too bad. Maybe this is all a scare tactic.

With a sigh, he rises and vanishes behind me. I try to turn in an attempt to see. The back of the chair is too high. I turn back to the front. My mind races, as does my heart. Freezing cold water splashes over me. Dosing me worse than the other times. It's colder too. Or maybe it just feels colder since I was already cold. "Your name." His voice is louder. Rougher. My body shakes. Whether from fear or the cold, I can't be sure.

He comes back around and stands in front of me. A knife in one hand. A blindfold in the other. "Last chance." He says.

I want to talk. I do. Screw loyalty. A name will do no harm to anyone else. My body trembles so violently that I can't get my mouth to cooperate. Instead of speaking words, the only sound to escape is the chattering of my teeth as they rattle against each other.

The blindfold is placed over my eyes. The lack of sight heightens my fear. I don't want to die. I don't want to be tortured. Still, my body doesn't cooperate to give my captor the answers he desires.

The pressure of a blade against my shoulder startles me. I involuntarily jump, causing the blade to pinch my skin further. I can feel the skin break. It isn't deep. It's a threat. No. A promise.

A door opens. It sounds close and a new voice speaks. It's male, authoritative. "She still not talking?"

The blade leaves my skin as my captor speaks. "Not yet." He takes a few steps, it sounds like he's circling around me. I swear I even hear him sigh in disappointment.

Is he upset he was interrupted during our torture session?

The press of the blade returns, only this time it is on my other shoulder. "But, she will." He says.

Footsteps approach. The new man is getting closer. "Has she said anything?"

"No."

"Stubborn." The new guy states.

"Or loyal."

Yes loyal. I am loyal. Though I am definitely reconsidering my loyalty and I sure as hell will not be assisting my dad with any other missions. Not ever. I try again to speak. My body can't cooperate.

"But to who? Is it the Irish?" I internally scoff. As if. They haven't recovered from the last war. "Russian?" They pause. As though contemplating.

Russian? I thought they were Russian. Are they messing with me? Is this a trick to get me to talk?

"Or is she working for Ramirez? A female operative seducing men into spilling secrets in the bedroom sounds like a Cartel trick." Ponders the new male.

I am definitely not Cartel. Though they do have the seducing men into spilling secrets part partially right. Not the bed part. I never got undressed or into any beds. My job was to get the men alone and away from other people. Sometimes it was back alleys, parking lots, or the occasional hotel room. Each time my father was there and waiting. He would knock the men out and take them to wherever he takes them to do whatever it is he does to get them to talk.

I had never wanted to be involved in that part. Though right now, I'm not only learning what it would be like, I'm experiencing it. With whatever luck I possess my experience has still been mild compared to what I know awaits me the longer I refuse to speak.

The knife lifts from my skin again as my captor speaks. "We can bring Ramirez in and find out."

"Do it." Says the man I'm now assuming is the boss.

Fuck.

CHAPTER SIX

Massimo

I hate leaving her in such a vulnerable state. Blindfolded, practically naked, cold and now wet. I shouldn't hate it. She could still be the enemy. Regardless, I shake my head in an effort to empty the thoughts in my head and then turn to leave the room and retrieve Ramirez. He is down the hall in a soundproof room. He is beaten and bruised. When someone is strapped down in this room, it is typically the last room that they ever see. One of our enforcers is working him over. We've gotten little from him. It's barely been 24 hours since we captured him. If he is anything like me, he won't crack. He would rather die than betray his men.

In a warped way it makes me respect him. Even with me being the one who will end him. I unlock him and grab him under one arm and signal my enforcer to do the same. We let his feet drag across the ground as we move into the room with our other guest.

Her blindfold still in place. I can see her body clenched tight from the suspense we have left her in. Clearly she's nervous about what is about to happen. I'm sure by now she can smell Ramirez's rancid body odor. It's a mix of blood, sweat, and urine.

Luca has a second chair waiting for us. It will allow our guests to face each other directly under the bright light. Luca and I have done this a time or two. We will stand in the shadows and ask questions. See if either gives any signals to the other. Signals of recognition, deception, and a slew of other tells.

Ramirez gets strapped in and his gag removed. He likes to bite when given the opening. That and spit. Our enforcer pauses to look at our guest. I haven't allowed him time with her. His methods are effective and everlasting. I had hoped to avoid that with her. If this proves pointless, I will have no choice but to tag in Elena. Her pain will be no less severe at her hands, but my conscience feels better letting a female handle a female. His pause has me wondering if he recognizes her. How long has she been in the field gathering intel? Have their paths crossed and we never knew? Or is he staring because she is a gorgeous near naked woman trembling and wet in our chamber?

I give him a nod and a stern glance. He knows the meaning. All my men do. It means he needs to back away. Move to a corner or wall and watch as a silent sentry.

Ramirez looks to me and smiles. "Have you brought me one last meal?" Disgust rolls through me. "She looks divine." He licks his lips. I see her trembling increase and she presses further into the back of her chair.

I punch him in the jaw. His head snaps to the side. "You don't recognize her?" I ask.

He smiles. His sadistic grin causing my teeth to clench. "Perhaps. It's hard to say. She's wearing too much and I can't see her full face."

This time Luca steps up and punches him in near the same place I did. Good. Fucker deserved it. Still, I'm pissed Luca beat me to it.

I move behind her and remove the blindfold. Her eyes are clenched and her head immediately ducks to the side. I can't allow it. I need them to see one another. I need to read their instinctual reactions upon first glance. I grasp her chin more harshly than I meant to and turn her head to face him.

His eyes instantly burn. "You!" It is not a pleasant look. It is dangerous. He tugs at his bindings. "You cost me an entire shipment! You're the reason I'm here!" He's shouting. Thrashing violently.

"Good! I hope they beat the shit out of you. I hope they break every one of your bones, spill every drop of your blood, and brand you so deep the devil himself will recognize it when you get to hell. They were just kids. Innocent young kids you sick fuck."

Fuck! She has fire.

There's also no doubt that she's not acting, or lying. She really does hate him. And his fury is real. We still don't know her real identity or who she works for, but this knowledge gives me hope that she's an ally.

Wait. Shipment? Kids? Fuck. It was a human trafficking shipment. I punch him again. My knuckles are bleeding from the force of the impact. Ramirez is temporarily knocked out.

"Livy?" Whispers a voice in the corner. A moment later my enforcer steps forward.

Luca steps next to him and puts an arm out to stop him from getting closer. "You know her?" Asks Luca.

I look to the girl. She looks shocked. Frozen even. She's not blinking. I'm not sure she's breathing.

"She's my daughter." Replies our enforcer. Holy Fuck!

"What?" Say Luca and I nearly simultaneously. His jaw

hits the floor. My eyes flick between my enforcer and her.

The enforcer, Raphael, moves closer to her again. Ignoring Luca's arm that now falls limply to his side. "Dad?" Says the woman. Her voice shaky.

"Liv. What happened? I've been looking for you for days!" He rushes to her and begins to free her from her the chair. I grab his shoulder and pull him back.

"Not so fast. She's here for a reason. We don't know if we can trust her."

"Of course you can. She's my daughter." He retorts. The ice in his voice clear.

"And she has been seen with members of every major crime family. She's up to something. And she isn't leaving until we find out what, and only if we deem she isn't a threat."

"Threat? She's not…She's not a threat. She would never do anything to harm the family. She's loyal." His voice now pleading. He knows the rules we live by. Threats are exterminated.

"That has yet to be seen. She hasn't exactly been cooperative thus far."

Her voice breaks through our standoff. I turn to face her. Her shoulders are slumping. Her lips and fingertips blue. Fuck. She's too cold. Her body is going into shock. "Because I didn't know who you were." Her words come out broken and almost garbled. "First rule, trust no-one you don't know. Second rule, never betray the family." She takes a deep, ragged breath. I rip off my suit coat and wrap it around her as I bend to undo her ankles, her father undoes her wrists.

Luca steps forward. "You refused to speak because you didn't know we were family?"

"Yes." Her word is barely more than a whisper. "Now I know. I'll tell you everything." Her last word fades as her head slumps to the side.

"Shit." Her dad shouts as he moves to grab her. I'm faster. I scoop her up into my arms. We need to get her to the infirmary. I stand with her in my arms. I take two steps to the door then stop. I turn to look at her father. "After the doctor has a look at her, you and I are going to be having a long conversation about what your daughter has been up to."

He nods his head and replies. "Yes sir."

CHAPTER SEVEN

Livianna

I wake in a warm bed. My body's still cold, but not nearly as chilled as I was. My head hurts, everything aches, and I'm struggling to remember how I got into this bed. Last thing I remember is being blindfolded and strapped to a chair. Awaiting the next step of my torture. Waiting for the moment it escalates to violence.

"Morning sweetheart." Comes a familiar voice at my side. I turn my head slowly. Squinting at the bright lights. "We haven't been formerly introduced. I'm Massimo D'Angelo of the Caruso Family." He gives me a smile. One I don't feel up to returning.

"Livianna Conti. Daughter to Raphael Conti, an Enforcer in the Caruso Family." I answer him out of respect for his position in the family. On a personal level I have no desire to exchange pleasantries. He may be hot as hell, but he can go to hell for all I care. His smile grows at my answer. It's not hard to surmise that he's pleased I am finally speaking to him.

"It's a pleasure to meet you Livianna." He stands from

his chair and moves closer to me. I wish he wouldn't. While he didn't physically put marks on my body he still subjected me to torment for days. I understand why he did it. He didn't know we played for the same team. Didn't know he could trust me. Now that that information is out in the open, I can see the regret in his eyes. A shiver wracks through my body. I pull the blankets up to my chin again and try to borrow further into their warmth.

I don't remember being brought to this room. Wait, what do I remember?

The jail cell, being kept awake, freezing cold water, a room of horrors, oh, and Julio Ramirez, that dirt bag. I hope he's still alive. Not because I have sympathy for him. No. The opposite. I want him to suffer. I want him to experience weeks, no months, of agony. It still won't be enough for the pain he's inflicted on others, but it would be a start.

The room isn't a hospital or infirmary like I had first thought. I am hooked up to an IV and have some monitors on me. The bed is too soft to be a recovery room bed. The sheets smell faintly of men's cologne. It's familiar but I'm having a hard time placing it.

My eyes flicker around the room. It's a large room. You could fit our whole trailer in here, with room to spare. The bed I am in is centered on the back wall. Windows sit to either side with small tables under each. There is a section of the room that looks like a lounge or mini living room. Another section has a kitchenette. It's large enough to cook some small hot meals. Speaking of food. My stomach rumbles loudly.

Massimo gives a chuckle. "I figured you'd be hungry when you woke up. I had some food sent up. Any preference?" He says as he stands and moves to the kitchen area. Looking again, I can see several trays on the small counter with metal lid coverings. He lifts one lid. The smell wafts across the room in seconds. Chicken noodle soup. Lifting another lid I'm hit with the smell of pancakes. Yes please!

Loading up his arms, Massimo brings both trays over and a bottle of water. Sets one tray on the side table, and the other on the bed beside me before handing me the water. "Doc set you up with an IV for fluids and nutrients. Weren't sure how long you were going to be out for, and since you'd refused to drink and barely ate downstairs, you were dehydrated."

"Wonder why that is?" I mumble under my breath. Then remember who I am in the presence of. I feel my face immediately redden. Shit. I need to apologize.

I open my mouth to apologize. He stops me with a lift of his hand. "Don't apologize. You can speak freely here. In fact, I demand it." He gives me a wink. Why? Is he flirting with me? Yesterday he was my captor. What is he now, a friend? A concerned boss? My brain hurts trying to understand. I'm still mentally tired from the lack of sleep.

Once I get some food in me, I hope I can go back to sleep. I know they want answers. Truthfully I want to give them and get out of here. Hopefully they will wait until I've rested some more before the new interrogation starts. Honestly, the information they will want, can be given by my father.

Speaking of. I'm mad at him. I was missing for two days. Two days. What the hell was he doing to find me that he didn't learn I was in the hands of his boss? When he realized I was gone and not coming back, shouldn't he have called the Don, begged for his help? If he had, he would have had to explain the situation. He would have told them I was helping with a job for him, and that I was taken from the bar. Massimo would have heard word of my father asking for help and made the connection.

My father was too surprised when he realized I was in the basement to have gone that course. So the question remains, what had he been doing to find me?

I cut through the pancake slowly. My muscles ache and scream in protest as I move. I'm able to get a few bites in before they cramp up and become useless on my lap.

I take a moment to evaluate my body's condition. I had been shaking from the cold in the basement before passing out. Was I in shock, or did my body shut down due to hypothermia setting in?

Massimo lifts the tray from my lap. He cuts a few pieces. I thought he was going to eat my leftovers. But he surprises me by lifting the fork to my lips. "I know you're still hungry. Eat." He says as he pushes the fork closer. I don't open. He sighs and lowers the fork a bit. "Look, I won't apologize for what happened. I had a job to do. It probably doesn't seem like it, but I went easy on you. I didn't want to hurt you. I did what I had to, and I'd do it again for the family."

If I had the energy I would laugh. Instead I open my mouth and allow him to feed me. "I understand why you did it. I would have too in your shoes." He freezes then turns away from the next piece of pancake he was cutting to look at me. "I didn't expect the ruthless and cold Enforcer of the Caruso Family to be sitting at my bedside hand feeding me breakfast."

He gives a nod. He's quiet for a moment. Taking the time to choose his next words carefully. "Three days ago, I wouldn't have."

"What changed?" I know curiosity killed the cat. I'm the cat in this situation. Yet, I need the answer.

"I met you." What?

Not the answer I was expecting.

He puts down the knife and fork. Stands and begins pacing by the window. "At first I didn't understand it. I felt drawn to you. I thought it was the mystery of who you were. As you know, we had heard rumor of a woman, a black widow of sorts being seen around town with various men from the different families. Each one found injured or dead hours later. When we realized that no one from our side had been touched, we grew curious. I had my team scattered across the city looking for you. We had no physical description so it was like finding a needle in a haystack. But we found you. Low and behold, you were seen with one of our men that night. It sealed your fate. I knew then that I needed to take you in." He pauses, stops his pacing, and resumes his seat in the chair by the bed. "I could see the strength in you that night. The fight you had in you. Instantly I respected you. And to be frank. I wanted you. Physically. I find you very attractive."

Damn. His confession has my stomach tightening and wetness pooling between my legs. I find him attractive as well. In another life, I might even have been willing to explore it. Not today. He just reminded me of a more important matter. The rat that got away. "You need to bring him in."

"Who?" Surprise overwhelms his face. I know I've caught him off guard. He was probably expecting me to jump his bones after his confession. Any other woman probably would have. He's hot as hell. I'm sure he's never hurt for female companionship. Losing my virginity to him definitely wouldn't be a horror story to remember. He's oozes confidence. He's the kind of man who knows how to please a woman. Momentarily I wonder if he'd be a gentle lover, or a beast in the sheets. Would he be concerned for the woman's pleasure, or just his own.

Shaking those thoughts and taking a deep breath to calm my libido. "Joe, Joseph, whatever you call him. My target. The one from the bar. You have to stop him."

"Joseph? Our soldier? What is it you think he's done?" Massimo looks angry. I was too when I found out. Though I don't think his anger is at Joseph. His dagger eyes are piercing me.

"Yes. Him. The one from the bar that night. He's a rat, and a bastard. My father will tell you. He's feeding information to Ramirez' men. He's been working with them for months. Getting in their good graces and helping with their trafficking business."

"And you know this how? He confess to you?"

"No. You interrupted us before he could." Again my mouth has no filter. Damn. Too bad I'm now past caring. That man is still out on the streets. Hunting young girls. Kidnapping them and trying to break them before selling them to the Cartel. Massimo looks skeptical. "Look, ask my father. He will tell you. It's why I was at the bar that night. I was targeting him. Dad found evidence that he was a rat. From my time with Ramirez' men, I knew someone from the Caruso Family was helping them with their...." I gulp. Not wanting to say it, but needing to. "Procuring of inventory."

"Again, how do you know it is him? What evidence do you have? Did you see him? Did he say something?"

I shake my head. Like I said we never got far enough for me to learn all his secrets. "I know. Talk to my father. Get him in your fun room and he'll sing like a canary."

"You want me to take your word for it?" He asks.

"Yes." I don't beat around the bush.

He scrubs a hand down his face. "What if you're wrong?"

"I'm not." I'm one hundred percent confident I'm not.

"How do you know?"

"I just do."

"If I'm going to trust you, I'm going to need more than that." He raises one eyebrow. It's a challenge. He doesn't trust me. I get it. I don't trust him completely either. I respect him. There's a difference.

"Fine. You want to know?" He nods. "I read it off him. I'm good at reading people."

"You read it off him?" Confusion coats his words. Yeah, confuses me too. It's hard to explain my gift.

"Yes. It's what I've been doing. I spent time with those men. Read their physical reactions to various mundane questions. Flirted, got them relaxed around me. A lot of what is unsaid is in the eyes." Massimo nods slightly. It's encouragement to continue. "I'm sure you are familiar with some of the tells. Yes? Shifting eyes or refusal to make eye contact when answering a question. Means they're lying."

"Yes." I knew he would be. It's the basics they are taught when training to be soldiers. It comes in handy. It's child's play compared to what I do. And what I do, can't be taught. Not to my level at least. That's not me bragging. It's a fact.

"I can read deeper than that. I see it in their eyes. See it in the way they stand, sit, walk, and talk. Most of the time it's not what they say, it's how they say it."

"And you know by spending what, twenty minutes at the bar with Joseph that he's a rat and working with the Cartel?"

"Yes." Massimo still doesn't look convinced. "Should I read you? If what I tell you is true, will you trust me?" I offer. It's gotten me in trouble in the past. I'm sure it will again now. I've already learned so much since sitting in this room with him.

"I'll consider it." He sits back with his arms crossed over his chest. His forearm muscles tightening. The veins bulging. Yum. Some women love a man's face, some his chest or ass.

Me. I like the arms. I want someone with strong arms to hold me tight. I want to feel safe, protected, cherished, in big burly arms.

Good enough. "Need to warn you. You might not like what I tell you. You'll probably be mad at me."

"Doubt it." He still doesn't think I know him at all. I think I know him better than himself. Or at least more than he is willing to admit about himself.

"I don't." I take a deep breathe. "You're an only child. You're left handed. But you shoot and attack with your right first. It's not instinct. It's technique. You know that everyone expects you to be right handed. It's more common. You do it so they don't anticipate the left. Leaves them unprotected and perfect for you to strike." His eyebrows raise and he unfolds his arms. Got his attention now. "You were recently promoted. That part is common knowledge. Congrats by the way." I throw that in to see how we reacts. Just as I thought. There is a tightening of his eyes and his left fist twitches like he wants to make a fist. "You aren't happy though. It's what you've worked for. You feel guilty about not being happy. You want to be Don. You want to be boss."

Fuck. Now I've pissed him off, just as I suspected. His eyes darken and he sits up straighter. "You don't want to feel this way. You love Luca like a brother. You are happy he's Don. You wouldn't want to take it from him. But secretly you wish it was you. You think that if your mother hadn't left that your father would have worked his way up to Underboss before Ricco." Smoke is now streaming out of his ears.

"How do you know about my mother?" His voice is deadly.

"I told you. I read people." He still doesn't believe me.

"Who told you?" He barks.

"No one." I can't help my instinct to shrink back at his

dark, menacing gaze. "Look around the room. There are no family photos, no knick knacks. You come from a broken home. There is no feminine touch. Everything is dark and muted. Means it was the mother who left. You aren't in a relationship. There are no signs of a woman in this room. The bed smells like you. Means you don't trust woman. Your mother cheated on your dad. You don't have anything expensive in here. Not even a large TV. You grew up poor, she wanted more. Dad didn't take it well. I'm guessing drinking. You take care of him."

"You've been spying on me!" He stands. Knocks his chair over.

"No." I throw my hands up. I knew he'd be mad. It's what always happens. "I told you. I read you. It's what I do. It's why I was helping my father."

"I don't believe you."

"I know."

"Then why try to sell this lie to me."

I sigh in defeat. Why can't I be normal? Why do I always manage to piss people off? We were getting along. He was treating me well. Finally. "It's not a lie. It's my burden. I told you, you wouldn't like what I told you. Believe me or not. I didn't lie. I even told you ahead of time, you wouldn't like what I would tell you."

Massimo glares at me for a few moments, then turns on his heel and storms to the door. He reaches out for the handle and pauses. "You are not to leave this room. A guard is posted outside."

"So I'm still a prisoner?" I already know the answer. No. But...

"I don't trust you. You'll stay here until I do, or until you are no longer being hunted."

CHAPTER EIGHT

Livianna

It's been two days. Two days of being stuck in this god forsaken room. Massimo hasn't come back. Food has been dropped off at the door, and the doctor came to remove my IV and check on me.

My anxiety is reaching new heights. I've never disliked being alone. It was safer. I couldn't offend people if they weren't around. Problem is. Now that I'm alone, all I can do is think.

Think about my father. How I came to be here. Massimo. Wondering what he is doing. Wondering if he is thinking of me. Wondering what it would be like to have a night with him. He isn't the relationship type. What kind of woman would it take to get him to settle down? Definitely not me.

My mind runs in circles. Never able to reach an answer that satisfies me. Then it goes back to the last thing he said before he stormed out. I'm being hunted. By who? I was caught by the Italians. Dad had me with men from all the other families, so I guess it's a toss-up. Who could I have pissed off more?

Honestly. All of them.

Men don't take kindly to being shown up by a female. Especially one they expected sex from and didn't get. It torpedo's their mood and royally pisses them off.

Lost in thought, I don't notice the door being opened. Or the three of them entering. I gasp in surprise as I do. My hand instantly flying up to my chest. It pisses me off. Not them coming in. But, me not being on guard enough to notice right away. Being lost in my mind isn't good. It's sometimes difficult to come back from. I tend to go down the rabbit hole and can't find my way out. Stuck thinking on the endless what ifs.

Luca approaches first. He motions to the couches. I follow his wordless instructions and take a seat on one of the armchairs. I sit on the edge. Not wanting to get too comfortable. Luca and the woman I'm guessing is his new bride, Elena, take a seat beside each other on the couch opposite me. Massimo stays standing. Like a silent sentry in the background. His eyes don't look at me. His familiar scowl present on his face. Damn. I liked it when he smiled. Will I ever see him smile again?

"Hello Livianna. It's a pleasure to officially meet you."

"You as well Don Luca." His eyebrows raise. It's not common knowledge that he has taken over the throne yet. My gaze flits over to Elena. I don't need to ask why they are here. I know. They want me to show them how I read people. They don't believe the story Massimo told them. How do I know this? I read it off of them. Skipping their well-rehearsed lines, I jump right in. Turning to Elena, I greet her next. "Nice to meet you Elena."

Her eyes widen in surprise. Luca's face flickers only slightly. Massimo prepared him for our meeting. He's trained to not show emotion. Just like Massimo. Only, it doesn't matter with me. To anyone else, yes, they hide it well.

"You know who I am?" She says. "How?"

"Word is that Don Bosco found his long lost daughter. She took over the marriage contract to Luca." I nod my head in his direction. "You are sitting closer than acquaintances, but not touching. You thought to be mindful of that. The giveaway is the faint indent on both your left ring fingers, but no tan line. A new ring you've worn until recently. You took them off so as to hide more of your identity. It won't help. Luca's itching to touch you. He's a man in love with you." I let my gaze roam over him. Slowly taking him in. "Obsessed actually. He doesn't like not touching you. Thinks you are going to run. He's already prepared to chase. In fact. If you look in his back pocket, he has a pair of handcuffs. You pissed him off this morning. He wants to link you to him, but hasn't done it yet. Didn't want to come in here like that. He's waiting until you walk out of here."

Elena's eyes widen further. Then she turns to Luca and shoves him hard. He falls slightly to the side. She caught him off guard. Her hands dive to his ass. Or pockets. Hard to tell from this angle. A clink of metal brings a smile to my face. It was a good guess on my part. Could have been zip ties, or another restraint. I went with cuffs because they can be padded, which his are. He wouldn't want to hurt his woman. It's sweet while being utterly ridiculous.

"Luca James Mariani! You will not cuff me again." She doesn't raise her voice. Not much. She doesn't have to. The tone says it all.

Luca's eyes flash from me to her. His mask has slipped off. He is wondering how much more I know. The answer will surprise him, I'm sure. "Then don't make me." He rebuts. There is no anger in his voice. Only care. It's sweet

60

and has me looking to Massimo. His eyes are on me. Still set in a glare, though softened slightly when he looks at his friend. He's happy for him. And jealous. Huh.

Before Elena can retort. I jump in again. I want this interrogation into my abilities over so we can move onto more important things. To do that I need them to believe the truth. "It's because of the blood." All three eyes turn to me. "I can smell the faint scent of copper and soap. You recently showered to remove the evidence. Both of you have. Luca's mad cause you crept down to the basement without him knowing." Elena's eye roam over her body. Most likely trying to see what I see.

"You missed some blood on the back of your pinky. Also, you're wearing thick socks and it's not cold in here. But it is in the basement. You spent time down their recently. You're also more relaxed than Massimo and Luca. Means you could have recently had sex, but you didn't because it would have been with Luca and he isn't showing the same markers. Which means you went with option two. You exercised. It wasn't at the gym. You don't look like you like to run in place, and hitting a bag isn't satisfying enough to you. You needed something real. Julio is still here. You paid him a visit. Luca's mad cause he was in a meeting. He's been having more of them and he hates the time away from you."

Massimo takes a few steps closer. His face still set in his mask. Luca on the other hand looks impressed. "Could have learned that by sneaking around the compound." Luca says confidently.

"You and I both know I haven't. You moved the guard from my door as a test. You wanted to see if I could be enticed to leave the room, and what I would do if I did. The cameras you have in the hallway and the one hidden in the bookshelf behind me would have alerted you if I left."

All three eyes dart to the camera. I pay attention to my surroundings when I'm not distracted. The morning I woke up, I cataloged the room. Yesterday after my shower, I noticed it changed. Found the camera a few minutes later. Didn't touch it. Just knew it was there.

"Seeing as I haven't left the room, and no one has come to speak with me, I would say it's safe to say, I had no way of knowing those details, now could I?"

Luca concedes first. "No. You couldn't."

"You believe her?" Asks Massimo.

"You don't?" Questions Elena as she turns to look at him.

He seems to mull it over for a minute. "No."

"Why not?" She asks.

"Could be good guesses, nothing more."

"I don't see how." Replies Luca.

I give Massimo a quick look. He needs more. Something concrete. Something that can't be a guess. I look him over until I see it. "You trust me. And you're mad about it. You just met me and you trust me. Something you don't often do. Especially not with women." I pause. Letting that sink in for a moment. "You have a woman in your life. One you wanted to trust. One you contemplated asking to marry you after Luca fell for Elena. You're happy for your friend and you feel ready to settle down too. But you haven't asked her. Haven't bought a ring either. You know what's stopping you. You just won't admit it. You don't trust her."

"Do so." Retorts Massimo defensively.

"No, you don't." I reply bluntly. "You don't have proof that you shouldn't and it pisses you off that you are second guessing yourself. You went to see her today. It didn't go well."

Luca turns to his friend. Eyebrows raised. "That's where you went?"

"Shut up." Massimo says to Luca.

"She tried to kiss you." I continue. This time it's Elena who looks at him.

Massimo smiles like he's won. "She did kiss me."

"You're right. She did. On the cheek." Massimo's eyes widen. Got him! "You have a faint smudge of lipstick near your ear. It's a partial mark. One you get from the quick turn of a cheek to avoid it being on the lips. You wouldn't let her kiss you. I'm guessing it's cause you felt guilty."

He crosses his arms over his chest. Trying his best to look smug. He still wants to deny what he knows to be true. He's almost cracked. "Why would I feel guilty?"

"Because she isn't who you wanted. You went there to fuck her. To get the thoughts of someone else out of your head." I don't break eye contact with him. He takes a few steps closer.

"Is that right?" He continues to get closer. He's stalking his prey. Me.

I nod.

"Tell me." He's in front of me now. Bending as he speaks so we are eye level. "Who was I thinking about?"

My eyes dart to his lips. They are slightly open. His warm minty breathe brushing my cheeks. I take a fortifying breath. "Me."

His lips crash onto mine. His hands dive into my hair. My arms go around his neck. Damn he can kiss. He steals the breath from my lungs while simultaneously breathing new life into me.

I'm not sure how long we spend kissing. Could be minutes, or hours. What I do know, is it wasn't long enough. We break apart when Luca clears his throat loudly. Judging by the growl that escapes Massimo's lips he is just as upset about being interrupted.

He pulls back his lips from mine as he places his forehead against mine. "You believe me now?" I ask.

"Yeah babe. I do."

I knew the answer but I like hearing it from his lips. Knowing he believes me and knowing he accepts the knowledge are two separate things. The latter is sometimes harder for me to read so hearing it from his lips and not detecting any signs of a lie reassures me and puts me at ease.

"You two can get back to sucking face later." Says Elena. There is a hint of joy in her words. The hint isn't only in her voice. Her face is radiating happiness. I'm betting her and Massimo have gotten closer in recent weeks and is happy for her husband's friend.

"Cock blocker." Huffs Massimo. There is no heat in his tone. It makes me turn to him.

He smiles and kisses me softly on the lips. "You pussy blocked me first." Snaps back Elena. I laugh. A deep belly laugh. One I haven't done in years. Three of them join me in laughing. It must be an inside joke between them and it feels good, feels right, that I was included in the moment.

"Keep your pussy and cock in your pants. We have work to do." Says Luca. His arm now draped over his wife's shoulders. The tender look he gives her as he kisses her temple melts my heart further. Then he turns to me. Massimo pulls me close, then has us falling to the chair I was previously seated in. Me now on his lap. His arm around my waist. Luca and Elena take up a similar position opposite us.

My body stiffens at first. I've never sat on a guy's lap before. Logically I know it's not meant to be sexual at the moment. My body, doesn't know that. It heats up at his touch. The circle his hand is rubbing on my thigh has my stomach coiling. I've had my share of moments where I felt desire. Where I felt the urge to seek male comfort. I never acted on it, and it was never this intense. How long will I last? Is that all Massimo is looking for? A bed warmer? What if he doesn't like how inexperienced I am. What if I'm not any good in bed?

Shit. Now my mind has gone down the rabbit hole. Massimo must see it. He gives my leg a pinch. "You still with us sweetheart?" The word has the affection it was missing previously. I soak it in and let myself relax further into his touch.

I intertwine our fingers and reply. "Yeah, sorry."

He smiles, raises our hands and kisses my knuckles. "It must be hell to be in your mind." He's not wrong. I also don't detect any malice in his tone.

"It can be. People don't like when I blurt out the truth they don't want to admit. I've had to learn to hide a lot over the years. Lost a lot of people who couldn't handle my words, or didn't like me having secrets when I didn't share."

"Understandable." Comments Luca. Damn, I almost forgot they were here still. "Please don't feel like you have to walk on eggshells around us. We welcome your honesty."

"Even if it upsets you?" They say they want me to be me now. How long will it last? I'm convinced they will change their mind. They haven't spent enough time with me.

Massimo squeezes his arm banded around me. "Yes. We know you aren't speaking to be vengeful. And we like honesty."

"Okay." I reply. I still don't believe this is what they want, but I'll go along with it. For now.

"Great." Says Luca. "Now, onto business. You said Joseph is our rat. Tell us what you know."

CHAPTER NINE

Livianna

For hours the three of them questioned me. I told them everything I could. I didn't hold anything back. They seemed to appreciate my candor and honesty. It felt good to unload to someone who understood my burden. They too have things they can't share with anyone else. Private Mafia business needs to stay just that. Mafia business. Being at the top of the totem pole, there are only so many people that they can confide in.

Massimo and Luca are lucky they were friends long before they become Boss and Second. The two of them have a solid foundation that they can lean on when they need to. It's visible to anyone who pays attention. They talk, in partial sentences. Complete each other's thoughts. The cohesiveness is astonishing. Even to me, and that's saying something. I've observed people and interactions for as long as I can remember, and no one else's connection comes close.

You can also sense that things are changing with them. Not bad changes necessarily. You could call them growing pains. Luca now has Elena. He hasn't forgotten Massimo, and Massimo has accepted Elena as part of the pact. It's fun watching their playful banter. It's clear that she won his trust. She won everyone's.

She's also a badass. Slightly scary. Quick to whip out her knife. Which makes me flinch for mine. I've been keeping it in the pocket of the pants she lent me. They are a bit tight, but I've stolen one of Massimo's sweatshirts so I don't feel as self-conscious. I have a big ass. I know it. I'm not ashamed of it. But these leggings are unforgiving. The fabric is stretched to the point you can see the color of my underwear beneath them. They're pink. The sweatshirt is big on me and easily falls to mid-thigh so it hides my bum. Still, I've found Massimo looking. It brings a smile to my lips when I catch him. He has no shame, and I'm finding I like that about him. A lot.

After the meeting, I was exhausted. But Massimo and I still needed to talk. His parting words from the other day are still lingering in the back of my mind. I decided to broach the subject over dinner. He had pizza brought up to us. The two half eaten pies sit in front of us. I am done eating, while Massimo continued to graze. Now is the time.

"What did you mean the other day when you said I was being hunted?"

He sighs, and tosses his crust to the table. "I shouldn't have said it like that. We aren't even sure how much anyone else knows."

"Knows what?" I ask.

He pulls me onto his lap. I'm straddled his hips. My knees barely reach the cushion, his thighs are so thick. "About you. We know we aren't the only group that knew you were meeting with various members of the families in town. You pissed a lot of people off."

Shit. I knew that would happen. I wanted to slow down the jobs. Spread them out more. They wouldn't have been able to find connections as easily if I had. I did my best with the parameters I was given. Wore tons of make-up and dramatic eye shadow and liner. A slutty wardrobe that differed completely from my usual, casual, covered attire. I know in the grand scheme of things they aren't significant changes and if anyone knew me they could tell it was me without difficulty. At the time it still made me feel better. Now, not so much.

"What's going to happen?" I try to keep the panic out of my voice.

"We need you to stay here." He says. His words sting. They are a reminder of my first few days here. I don't really have the desire to run. I like Luca and Elena. And I really like Massimo and want to see where our attraction will take us. It might not be forever. That idea hurts more than I thought it would. Could he and I have a forever?

"So, I'm still a prisoner. A captive in a new cell." I lean my forehead against his.

He sighs. "I don't want you getting hurt. You're free to roam the compound. You don't have to stay in this room, or this house. Just please don't leave the grounds. Luca, Val, and I are gathering intel. Trying to see if anyone has identified you. We have some allies out there. When we explain the circumstances, and expose the rats you found in their organization it should smooth things over."

That plan sounds promising. "What about school? I have class. I've already missed too many lectures."

He doesn't answer. His mouth closes tightly. He's hiding something. Something he knows will piss me off. "Tell me." I demand.

Massimo's hands grip my hips tightly. It's like he's trying

to keep me from leaping off his lap. The gesture doesn't help me remain calm. If anything, I'm more alert to his tells. "I called the school. They've given you a leave of absence."

I try to jump, just as he predicted. I don't want him touching me right now. I don't want his affection. How dare he! I may not be a book nerd, or a scholar, but I liked school. I liked learning even if I hated studying. "How could you? Why would you do that? I'm supposed to graduate in a month." No, no, no. I've worked too hard. I promised my mother I would go to college. I need to graduate. I promised.

His hands move to my back. I can see he wants to pull me closer to him. I read his intention and use his loosened grip to escape his grasp. My feet carry me over to one of the windows. I stare out it without really seeing.

I can feel his presence behind me before I hear him. He's creepy quiet when he wants to be. "I won't apologize."

"Of course not." I scoff. I'm sure he can count the number of times he's apologized in his life on his hand.

He wraps his arms around me and spins me to face him. "I need to keep you safe. Do you get that? Do you feel this?" He takes my hand and moves it to his chest. His heart is beating quickly. "I've never felt this way before. I get we don't know each other well. If you were anyone else, I would have fucked you and left you already." My eyes widen at his blunt honesty. "I don't want to do that with you. I don't want you to be a one and done. I want to see what the future can hold."

"You want a future with me? You want to do the whole dating, marriage, and babies?" I realize too late what I said. Who the hell mentions marriage and babies after a day of dating? Are we dating? Do we have a title? Does he want a title?

"Stop thinking." He boops me on the nose. It's effective.

It draws me out of my head.

"Did you just boop me?" I ask with a laugh.

He smiles. "I did. Needed you back with me. You can escape into your mind later." He gives me a kiss on the forehead then continues. "You already know I haven't trusted many people in my life. Even fewer are women. I trust Greta, Luca's mom, and now I trust Elena. That was it." I should feel offended he didn't mention me, but I know he's not done sharing. "And now I trust you. Like you said. I didn't want to. My gut was telling me to trust you, and I normally trust my gut. With everything that has happened, all the rats Elena uncovered, I wasn't sure anymore if I could trust it. So I kidnapped you and tried to get you to talk. When you refused, it made me fear the worst."

"You realize, you could have avoided that whole horrid thing, if you had just introduced yourself. I would have asked to speak to Luca or Bosco to see you weren't lying. I knew their faces. I didn't know yours. The conflict would have been over before it started."

"I wasn't thinking. I reacted. Saw you flirting with a guy. I got jealous. I didn't understand why at the time. It was my gut. It knew I wanted you."

"Even then? When I could have been the enemy?" I ask.

"Yeah." He gives me a kiss. A soft peck. I want more. Now is not the time. "Even then."

"Would you have ever acted on it?" I'm not sure I want to know the answer.

His expression shifts for a moment. I know he doesn't like letting his mask slip. "I would have made a convincing argument to get you to leave with me. Then I would have fucked you and left you before you woke up in the morning."

I was right. I don't like his answer. He must see the hurt on my face. I don't mask it. He told me to be myself. So I will.

"Great."

"Hey." He lifts my chin with a finger under it and applying slight pressure. "I'm glad that's not the case. We didn't get off on the right foot. But I want to do this right. I want to try dating you."

"Try?" I tease.

He gives a little laugh. "Yeah. Never dated exclusively before. Been on only a handful of dates in my life. Never a second one. Never had a girlfriend. Never had a woman in my bed here."

I look to the bed on our left. "Never?"

He kisses my temple. "Never. Never wanted anyone enough to try. Never thought I could trust a woman enough."

"You trust me enough?"

"Babe. Sweetheart. You thought I was Russian and refused to speak. You held every secret that could hurt our family even when I was a cruel bastard to you. I humiliated you, degraded you, and made you lose consciousness for a day while fighting hypothermia. Still you were adamant not to break. Not to save yourself. Not to save your father. You did it for the family. The one that didn't even know you worked for them. That puts you at the top of my list of trustworthy people." He kisses me again. Deeply this time.

I throw my arms around his neck. He responds with a chuckle before lifting me up by the back of my thighs. My legs wrap around hips. His erection digging into my pelvis. I rock to get more friction. It feels so good. I can't help but to moan into his mouth.

This is it. Tonight I'm losing my virginity. To this man. My man. I don't care if we only date for a week, a year, or forever. Tonight he is mine and I am his.

His hands give my ass a squeeze. "Love this ass." He whispers huskily as his lips move from mine and down my

71

neck. The sweatshirt must be in the way, because he rips it off of me. Then his hands are back on me. I didn't wear a shirt underneath. Just my pink lace bra that matches my panties. He growls as he pinches my nipple through the fabric. It hardens into a stiff peak at his touch. "So sensitive." He growls before sucking the other one into his mouth. The added friction of the lace with his tongue against my flesh has my hips pumping against his. Riding him through our clothes.

In the next second, I am airborne. Falling to the bed and watching him rip his own shirt off of his body. Damn.

The man is a god. Built like he was hand chiseled. Deep definitions separate each ab. The elusive V that makes women all over the world drool has me clenching my thighs tight to get some relief from the ache that's building in me. Moving my eyes lower, I freeze on his bulge. I can see the large outline of his cock through his tight jeans. Oh fuck. He is huge. He won't fit.

His hands land on my calves and he uses the grip to pull me to the edge of the bed. "Need you naked." He says as he tears off my leggings.

"You too." I murmur as I reach for his belt. He pulls it free and drops it to the floor. His hands push mine away from his zipper. It's for the best. My hands have begun to shake. I can't tell if it's from nerves, excitement, or a combination.

A combination. I'm going with that. I am nervous. Horribly so. I always wondered if I was attractive naked. I mean. I personally don't think I'm bad looking. But from a male perspective. Am I desirable? With the way Massimo's eyes have burned with heat and want since he took off my sweatshirt, I would say he likes what he sees. Loves it even.

His gaze continues to eat me up. His tongue licks his lips

like I'm his favorite treat, and he's about to gorge himself on it.

Yes please! I've never had a man's mouth on me. I am very excited Massimo will be the first. If things go well. He may be the only.

That thought sends a shiver through me. A shiver of excitement. Contentment. Yeah, I want Massimo forever. He is loyal, strong, and gorgeous. He isn't easy to read at times which I like since I find people in general too easy to read. I would get bored in a relationship if I could judge their every action and reaction before they even know their choice. I know I won't have that problem with Massimo. I had wondered when I first felt the attraction for Massimo, if he would be capable of being affectionate. Could he be a gentle lover and a cuddler in the after moments? I'll be finding out soon.

I'm betting he will be. I don't think he is with everyone. Past hook-ups, definitely not. With me, yeah. It's the hungry look in his eyes. The flexing of his hands like they are fighting to keep off of me. And the urgency of his lips on my lips and skin.

Massimo's eye remain locked with mine as he pops the button of his jeans, then begins to tease the zipper down. Damn, he has me hot and bothered. Not even naked yet and I am about to combust.

Suddenly a loud shrill noise echoes around the room. It breaks our eye contact. The heat gone from his eyes. Massimo quickly does his jeans back up and walks away. I try not to over think his actions. His phone is ringing. That is all. It's nothing I did.

Still, I find my hands grabbing at the covers to pull them over and cover me up. Massimo has moved to the couch and answers the call. His voice is low. He talks for a minute before he sends a quick worried glance my way. "Be right down." He says. Loud and clear enough for me to hear.

Without another word, or second glance, he moves to the closet and grabs a new shirt then leaves the room. Tears prick my eyes. He left. No soothing words or explanation. Just left me near naked on the bed.

Don't cry. Don't cry. I whisper repeatedly to myself as I crawl out from under the covers and retrieve my clothes from the floor. I redress quickly. I'm not sure how long he will be gone. Even if it's only a moment, I don't want him coming back see me sitting and waiting in the same position. I refuse to appear desperate.

I thought he wanted it. Wanted me. With how quickly he was able to walk away. No words, no parting kiss, I'm second guessing every action. Am I just a convenience to him?

I make myself busy cleaning up dinner in an effort to occupy my mind. After dinner is clean, the kitchen is spotless, the bathroom scrubbed, and the sheets of the bed changed, I run out of things to do. I don't have my phone, and Massimo has no TV in here. There are a few books and magazines. I comb through them as slow as possible, trying to draw them out.

Even they don't help time pass quicker. Finally I decide to get out of the room. It's late, and I don't know the Compound grounds well enough to navigate them at this hour like I want to. The fresh air sounds amazing. Instead, I find myself on the main floor, heading towards the kitchen. I was there earlier today with Elena when we took a break to eat lunch and the guys checked in on the men and other business.

On my way, I hear the muffled sounds of two people talking. It's hard to tell what they are saying, or who they are from this distance. Curiosity gets the better of me, and I creep as quietly as I can to the archway that leads to the living-room. I stick to the shadows. Not wanting to be seen. I'm glad I did, because the scene before me shatters my heart.

Massimo is on the couch. With a woman. I can't see her whole face. It is blocked by his head. She has dark brown hair, almost black. She is skinny and wearing a form fitting little black dress. She is gorgeous and appears every bit the vixen I had tried to emulate when I went on my missions. While mine was a ruse and a false embodiment, her appearance seems natural. She oozes sex appeal. I can see why Massimo came down to her. Their hands are grasped intimately. Their legs touching from hip to toe. Their upper bodies turned to face one another.

It is clear to me that this is not their first meeting. They have been intimate before. And if she is in his arms, on the couch at the compound, looking comfortable, she has been here before. Did he lie to me? Is she his girlfriend? Has he brought a woman here before when he said he never did?

The woman takes a hand and runs it along his jaw. I can't watch anymore. He didn't bat her away. Didn't stop her in anyway. Just hours ago he was kissing me, stripping me down, telling me he wanted to try with me, making me wish for things that I now know I had no business in believing.

I back-up slowly, going deeper into the shadows and continuing on to the kitchen. I was a fool. An idiot. I am so mad at myself. I scour the cupboards. I have no idea what I am looking for. I give up and just grab a glass of water. Sipping it slowly, my back leaning against the counter. My only light is that of the moon trickling in through the window.

All is quiet for a few minutes, until I hear the unmistakable click of a high heel on the marble in the hall. I set my glass down and noiselessly make my way out into the hallway.

It's a bit harder to see in the shadows and it takes a moment for my night vision to adapt. When it does, I see two figures. One female figure is hunched down. Inspecting the lock. No, not looking. She is picking the lock. Within moments she is successful. The door opens, and she enters. The second person, a large male enters with her and shuts the door behind him.

I get to the door and don't hesitate to enter. For a moment I wonder were Massimo is. Why did he leave this woman? Who is the man she is with? By the way his head had been twisting like on a swivel you could tell he was playing lookout. It was safe to say he wasn't a regular visitor to the compound, and definitely not one who was allowed to be here.

I don't have time to think too much further. I have a new mission. Find out who the hell this woman and man are and why they are breaking into the basement.

Getting to the bottom of the stairs, the hair on my arms and neck stands up. I am face to face with the cell I was kept in when I first arrived. A chill runs over me.

No time. No time for this. Need to find out what this woman is doing.

I creep further down the hall, passing the room of torture devices. The door is open and the room is clear. There is a faint light on at the end of the hall. I make my way to it. I hear voices and grunts. Inside, the mystery woman has Ramirez unchained. He is swaying on his feet. She is holding his arm over her shoulder. Supporting some of his weight.

Shit. I need a weapon. They can't get Ramirez out of here. He can't be allowed on the streets again. I run back down the hall. Not caring if I make noise. I am between our mystery guests and the only exit. I rush into the torture room and grab the first gun I see. Checking the clip, I ensure it is loaded. I grab a knife off the table as well. It is a serrated hunting knife. Then I rush back out while remembering to lock the door on my way. It should prevent them from also getting a weapon, or at the least, slow them down if they try.

Going back to the room. Ramirez is now being supported by the man. The woman is helping him to put on a shirt. I can see the bruises and cuts all along his torso. Good. I would take a minute to cheer. I can't.

"Don't move." I say as I step into the room and make my presence known. I raise the gun and lock its focus on the woman. She is probably the least dangerous to me. I realize it too late. I can move the gun, but my heart won't let me. It sees this woman as competition. I can't let her have Massimo. Not his heart, body, mind, nothing. It belongs to me.

I hope.

The woman turns so she is facing me head on. I recognize her. I've seen her around town. "I know you." She says with a smile. "You're like me."

"I'm nothing like you."

She takes a step closer to me. I click off the safety. She stops walking. "You sure? You use your beauty to get things. Get men to trust you with your curves. Then fuck them and steal any info you can grab."

Fuck this bitch. I fire a warning shot. I miss the woman. Not by much.

The stranger and Ramirez are long forgotten. The woman screeches and rushes at me.

CHAPTER TEN
Massimo

The sound of a gunshot echoes down the hall and into Luca's study.

"What the fuck?" He growls.

What the fuck is right. Who in god's name is firing at us? There is no consistent fire. It's not an ambush. No alarm at the gates, or compound walls have been activated. They are online and working.

Val clicks something on his computer while I run to the door to look down the hall. The gunfire came from somewhere in the house.

"Fuck." Screams Val as he jumps from his chair and runs out the room. "Basement. Now." He yells back at Luca and I. We give each other a quick glance before taking off after Val. Another shot rings out. We're closer. That definitely came from the basement. There is only one prisoner down there. Ramirez. Fuck. Did he get loose?

As I sprint through the halls, a stream of light followed by the flicker of a shadow catches my eye. The front door is open. Someone just went outside. More men are barreling down the stairs. I find Al in the crowd. He is a trust man who has been Luca's bodyguard and driver for years. "Put us on lock down. Find out who just left." I barely slow long enough to ensure he heard me.

He nods and runs out the door. With that handled, I continue down the hall, through the basement door, and down the stairs. I smell blood. Fresh blood. I run past a multitude of rooms and make it to the end of the hall. Ramirez's room. Bolting inside, I am stopped when I crash into Luca's back. I bite back a growl.

The room is twenty feet by twenty feet. Dead center is a ten foot by ten foot cell. A single chair is usually in the middle. It has been kicked to the side and broken. Two woman are inside the cell. They are rolling on the ground. Each trying to get the other hand. Who the hell are they? Where is Ramirez? How did they get here?

I go to step up to the cage. Ready to rip the door off. It's locked. I can see the keyring sitting in the center of the cell. Dangling over the drain. Fuck, we have a spare but it's upstairs, somewhere in Luca's new office. We haven't had to use it. The key is always on the wall outside the locked door to this room.

"Mass..." Luca whispers. I barely hear it. He says it just as the two women look up. I recognize them both immediately. My Livianna, and that bitch Rachel. The one I broke up with. The one Livianna knew I was tempted to do something stupid with. That stupid thing being propose marriage. Fuck am I dumb. Rachel is a lying bitch.

She stormed the gate this evening demanding to talk to me. That's the phone call that ripped me away from Liv earlier. I couldn't look at her. I wasn't sure what my facial expressions would say. I didn't want her to worry. As soon as

I got downstairs I realized I probably had confused and worried her more by just leaving the way I did.

I had meant to make things quick. Remind Rachel we were over. That we had no future. Then escort her out and tell the guards to notify everyone that she was not welcome here.

I made the mistake of allowing her into the compound. Instantly her hands were on me. Trying to rip my clothes off. I pushed her off and grabbed her hands and held them in her lap so she couldn't claw at me further. Then I sat her down and explained to her that I had no feelings for her. I have someone in my life. Someone I am committed to dating and being faithful too. She started with the waterworks. I went to get a tissue. When I got back to the room she was gone.

Her car, no longer at the front door. So I headed for the stairs, where I ran into Luca. He said Val had woken him because he found something on Joseph. We were still looking for the fucker. We were still talking when we heard gunfire.

What is she doing down here? Why is Livianna here and not in bed? Did she come looking for me? Did she see me with Rachel? Was she helping Ramirez?

No. Absolutely not. She hates him. There was no faking the disdain she showed for him. And he got mad at her upon seeing her. He hadn't talked since being brought in by us. Yet seeing her and he was foaming at the mouth. Yeah, they had history, not good history. She wouldn't free him. Sneak down to kill him, maybe. I wouldn't blame her is she did. I'd have rather she didn't as he deserved to suffer long and hard.

"What the fuck?" I can't stop the words from leaving my mouth.

Rachel begins to laugh. She has the gun in her hand. Liv is fighting for control of it. "Hey handsome? Looking for round two so soon?"

Livianna freezes. Disgust, hurt, and anger all visible in her eyes. Yet she doesn't relax her fight for the weapon. Good girl. Keep fighting. "Fuck no. I was trying to throw your ass out to get back to my woman."

The pain immediately vanishes from Livianna's face. She believes me. We both breathe a sigh of relief. I'm sure I'll get an earful about the situation later. In fact, I look forward to it. Right now, I just need my girl safe. Both Luca and I have our guns out and ready. There is no clear shot. The woman are moving too much.

We need the door open to help. Livianna senses it too. She uses her feet to kick at the key. "No." Shouts Rachel. She throws herself over Livianna towards the keys. Liv goes with her. They topple together. A mess of limbs thrashing then a loud pop. Gunfire. It echoes around the room. A fresh scent of blood rises.

"Liv!!!!" I scream and tear at the door of the cell. It creaks and groans. "Livianna!" There is no answer. Luca joins me at the door, so does Val and a few other men. A few collective yanks later and the door rips free. I sprint forward. "Call the doctor." I don't know if one or both are hurt or dead. If it's Rachel I don't care. But I can't lose Livianna. I only just found her.

Rachel's body is on top. I pull her off, none too gently. Luca takes her. There is a large pool of blood on her shirt, as well as all over Liv. She is face down. I don't want to move her. What if I hurt her more? What if she's bleeding from the chest and not flipping her over causes her to bleed out?

Fuck.

Fuck.

Fuck.

"Luca. Help me." Emotion claws at my throat. My words like a plea to my friend. I need him right now. Not just with moving her gently. I need his support. I need to know how to handle the emotions flowing through me. I'm not good with them. Anger and rage I know. Lust I am familiar with. Love. No.

Love.

Fuck. I love Livianna. I don't give a shit that I haven't known her long. I don't care if it's too soon, or even if she doesn't love me. Tough shit. I'm claiming her. She's mine.

As long as she's okay. If she's not, I don't know what I'll do. I suspect nothing good. My limbs buzz with the desire to kill. To pillage those who had any small hand in this moment. My vengeance will make Elena's look like child's play. I have kept the beast within me locked up. If Livianna is dead, I won't have a hope of holding him back.

Luca holds her head as I grab her torso and turn. Val is with us, moving her legs so we can place her on her back. She lets out a groan. Her eyes are closed. A hole in her shoulder. It's still bleeding. I rip off my shirt and press it to her wound. I need to stop the bleeding.

Paolo, one of our guards who ran down with us, stands from his crouch by Rachel. He looks me in the eye and shakes his head. "She's dead." Keeping my hands on Liv, I look to Rachel. A large gaping wound, soaked with blood sits in the middle of her chest. Looking down at Liv's hands, I see the gun dangling from her fingers. She pulled the trigger.

Fuck!

I must push too hard on her wound, as she lets out another groan of pain. This time her eyes open slightly. "Hurts." Her voice is barely a whisper. It's scratchy like she's struggling to speak. Fuck, if it isn't music to my ears.

"Sweetheart. I've got you. Doc's going to patch you up ok?"

"Kay." She says. Her voice trailing off. Eyes closing up

again.

I don't like it. I need her awake. I need to know she's still with me. "Liv. Keep those pretty brown eyes on me."

"No. Tired." God I love her. The personality she hid and squashed behind a false facade is coming out. I can't wait to see the real Livianna. I know I am going to love every piece of her. I already do.

"Liv." Says Luca. "I know you're hurt. Can you tell us where Ramirez is?"

Her eyes shoot open. "Shit." She looks around frantically? "Where are they?"

"Whose they?" Asks Luca.

"Ramirez and the guy. The one she came with. They were just here." Her voice sounds frantic. I don't want her panicking. It will raise her blood pressure. And she's still bleeding. I need her calm.

"What did he look like?" Asks Val. He has moved closer to her shoulder. The one opposite me.

Her breathes are shallow. I don't like the change. "Where is the Doctor?" I growl.

"Thirty seconds." Responds Paolo.

"Luca's height." Few inches short than me. "Muscular like Mass." I smile down at her and kiss her forehead. I know she loves my muscles. She's been checking them out every chance she gets. If I could, I would stay naked all day long just for her. Hell, I've already been adding weights during my gym sessions each day to keep my bulk. If she likes them, I'll keep them. Forever. I'll be the buffest ninety year old man if it means she is happy and continues to ogle me. "Dirty blonde hair. Late twenties I think. And Cartel gang tattoo on back of right hand. But he also had the Street Soldiers Gang tattoo on his left wrist. Both looked new…"

God I love her brain. I know she struggles to accept that

she thinks different. Notices things others don't. In situations like this, it's no burden. It's a fucking God send.

Street Soldiers were supposedly exterminated years ago. If they are back, then they are working underground. We'll need to get someone undercover with them. Someone we can trust to not be turned.

My eyes shift to Paolo. He must know what I am thinking. He has gone undercover for us before. His job with us keeps him inside the Compound. He guards the basement dwellers so his identity isn't known to outsiders. He is also a third Mexican and speaks Spanish fluently. His grandmother crossed the border illegally. Made her way to Chicago and fell in love with a Soldier. His family has been with us ever since.

"Good job Liv. That will help me find him." Soothes Val. He's also good with emotion. He's comforting my girl. Knowing she is upset at losing Ramirez. Not that it's her fault. It's the guards at the gate. They will be punished accordingly. They let Rachel in before I gave approval. They must not have check her car either for stowaways or weapons if she had help and a gun.

My mind is racing. My heart ready to beat out of my chest.

The doctor finally arrives. I step back to let him attend to Livianna. Luca stands as well. He takes the two steps towards me. My eyes never leave Liv's. "Stay with your girl."

"We need to find Ramirez." I retort. I want to capture and kill the bastard. Rachel got off too easy. She played me. Was it all a lie? How long had she been working with them. I had met her by chance at a bar months ago. I didn't have Val look into her, because she was supposed to be like all my other fucks. A one and done.

Only she wasn't. I was feeling exceptionally lonely. My

father was no longer sober even when I visited. His health is declining. I wanted someone to talk to. Someone who didn't know my whole story. I thought that could be Rachel. I never did open up to her. It didn't feel right. It should have been a sign.

"And we will." Replies Luca. His hand on my shoulder giving me a squeeze. "Val and I will get to work on it. You need to be with your girl."

I keep staring at Liv. The doctor is asking her questions. She's answering. Her eyes still locked with mine. It's keeping me calm. She must know it, because even when she winces in pain, her eyes don't waver.

The beast in me roars. I let her down. I allowed her to get hurt. "What do I say to her? How to make this better? She got hurt because of me. She killed because of me. She was innocent."

"It doesn't matter what you say. You'll know. The words will come." His hand leaves my shoulder and he heads towards the door.

"How?" I finally tear my eyes from Liv and plead with my friend. I can't mess this up anymore. I can't lose her. I can't lose anyone else.

"Just be there. Be with her. Talk to her. Tell her about yourself."

"I'm fucked up." It's the truth.

"Aren't we all?" He says with a smile. He leaves, taking Val and a few guards with him.

I turn back to the doctor, he has Liv's shoulder stitched up and a bandage over it. "Bleeding has stopped. It was a through and through, no major veins, arteries, or bones were hit. It will take a few weeks to heal and she should be in a sling to keep it immobile during that time. I want to move her. Get her to the infirmary side." Meaning the other half of the basement that we keep separate. "I want to get her on an IV for pain for at least the next twenty-four hours."

I nod. Move to Liv's side and squat down. "Going to pick you up now Sweetheart. Promise I won't drop you."

She gives me a lazy smile. "Thank you Mass. Thank you for coming after me."

She shouldn't be thanking me. I put her in danger. If she stays with me, she will have a target on her back. I should send her home. Get her away from me.

I pick her up as gently as I can. She bites on her lip. I know she is holding back the cry of pain. Kissing her forehead as I make my way out of the room and out of the basement. I make a promise to myself. To her. I will protect her. I won't be letting her go. I can't. I'll teach her to shoot, to fight. I'll get her a guard. Ten guards. I'll put a tracker in her arm. I'll stalk her wherever she goes. I don't care. I'm keeping her.

CHAPTER ELEVEN
Livianna

I'm not sure how long I was out for. There is an IV in my right arm that's feeding me some kind of pain killer because I'm not feeling much of anything at the moment. Well, not physically anyway.

Mentally I'm in anguish. I killed someone. It was a split second decision. We had been struggling with the gun for a while. I was losing strength. She had already shot the gun twice during our struggle. I knew if she did it a third time, it would be the end of me. So I used the keys as a distraction, got her to hurdle over me. The force of our changing weight sent us vaulting forward. With the gun at my shoulder, I prayed I'd miss the artery and fired. I knew it was a risk. But waiting was no longer an option. I couldn't get the keys to Massimo. They couldn't get into the cell. I couldn't get the gun out of her hands.

It was the only play I had to make. I knew shooting myself would hurt. I also knew there was a solid chance I would be killing her. The angle at which she was on top of me would have had the bullet enter her upper body no matter what.

I'm not mad she's dead. Good riddance.

In my missions for my dad. I had heard rumors of her. She was right to some degree when she said we were alike. Long before I was helping my dad and seducing men to get them to lower their inhibitions and lure them to my father, she was doing something similar. Only she was playing the long game.

First she did it with the Russians. She had worked her way into their fold and settled herself in as a mistress of the Pakhan, the Russian equivalent to a Don. While I had never met her, and I hadn't known our paths to cross, I knew of her. I hated her. She held no loyalty. She wanted money and power and did anything to get it. While I played a role, it was to keep the family safe. Hunt down the rat. Dig up dirt on those who longed to turn their backs on the Caruso Family.

How she ended up with Massimo, I'm not sure. I may not want to know.

I'm sure it involves them naked. I must physically flinch in addition to mentally doing so, because Massimo squeezes my hand tighter and calls out my name. "Liv. Sweetheart?"

I had felt his presence. Knew whose hand I was holding. I hadn't wanted to open my eyes. Opening them made it feel real. Made everything real.

"Come on baby. I know you're awake." He boops me on the nose. I guess it's our thing. The big scary Mafia Enforcer booping noses. I let out a little giggle at the image of him doing it to Luca or Paolo. I shouldn't have laughed. It jostles my shoulder and pulls at the stitches which sends a shot of pain up and down my arm. My eyes fly open and I let out a hiss. "Easy." He coos as he helps me to sit up and adjusts the pillows.

I use my free hand to rub at my forehead while I take stock of the rest of my body. Everything else feels okay. Guess the truth will come out after the IV is gone.

Massimo stands and strokes my hair. I'm not sure I want him close right now. I need to know who Rachel was to him. Did he love her? Why did he leave me to go to her?

I pull back from his touch. He sighs. His face showing his dejection. "You're mad" It's an observation not an accusation.

"Yes. I am. You left me." I need this off my chest. "I thought we both wanted to take the next step. You seemed into it, then you got a phone call and it was like I didn't exist. That hurt Massimo."

His mouth opens like he wants to interrupt, I don't let him. "You were gone for hours. All sorts of thoughts went through my head. And when I went downstairs to get a drink and clear my head, there you were. Holding her hands. Being close and intimate." Words are becoming choked. The emotions I want to hold back are fighting their way through.

"Sweetheart. I'm sorry. I wasn't thinking. I told you I've never been in a relationship. I've never had to think of someone else's feelings in a situation. Safety, yes. So, that's what I did. I know now I should have explained myself before leaving. I swear to you, I will communicate everything from now on." I don't answer him. I can see where he is coming from. He did tell me he had never been in a relationship.

Then again, even someone who hadn't, and who had seen the rejection and concern on my face when he gave me that singular look before he left should have been clue enough to talk.

"I swear. Nothing happened with her last night. I hadn't seen her since that day I broke things off and she tried to kiss me. It was her lipstick you saw on my cheek. Nothing happened that day either. I went over to her place cause she had called me a handful of times and wouldn't stop. I wanted her to know it was over. What she and I had was just sex, and it happened before I met you. Since then, I haven't been with her. Haven't been with anyone."

I nod my head. That gives me some level of comfort. I don't see any tells of deception or lying in his body language.

"Last night, she came to the Compound gate and was giving the guards hell. I'm not sure how she knew I was here. I never discussed the Mafia with her. I was attracted to her. Thought about dating her. Even went on one date so I could see if I felt a deeper connection. See if I could trust her." He looks so forlorn. I want to reach out and comfort him, but I don't. He needs this off his chest, and I'm not sure I'm ready for whatever this is between us.

I'm not sure I'm ready for this level of involvement in the Mafia. I wasn't comfortable with what I was doing with dad, but I did it for him. Now getting into a fight with Massimo's ex, getting shot, and killing someone, I don't know how to process all of this.

"My gut told me I couldn't. Guess I know why now. She was lying and using me the whole time. I'm so sorry sweetheart. You should have never had to face her, never had to fight her, or shoot anyone." An apology. Wow. "I want to say it won't ever happen again. I wish I could and mean it. My life is dangerous. With you as my woman, you will always have a target on your back."

"Massimo..." I want to tell him I'm not his woman. Not now, or yet, or maybe ever. After everything that has happened, I need to do some soul searching. I like Massimo. I could even see myself loving him. But this? This life of constant danger? Can I do that?

"I've already started taking precautions. You'll have a

team of guards when you're not at the compound. I'll train you. You look like you already know the basics of self-defense. I can teach you more. You may never need to use them, but you'll know them." He's up and pacing the room now.

"Mass…" I try again to interrupt him. He doesn't let me.

"Liv, you could have died. I almost lost you. Don't fight me on this. I'll be happy to fight about anything else. I'll even compromise on occasion. Not with your safety though." Finally he takes a breath.

"Come here." I hold out a hand for him. The same one he was holding earlier. His shoulders slump and he does as I asked. He grabs my hand and sits on the edge of the bed. "I like you Massimo."

The biggest smile I have ever seen spreads across his face. It squishes his cheeks and crinkles the corners of his eyes. He looks so relieved to hear those words from me. "I like you too. I really, really, like you."

"But, I can't be with you." The smile is gone. He rips his hand from mine.

He looks angry. "What do you mean you can't be with me?" There's an edge to his voice that he's never directed at me before.

I hate that I am doing this. I can't stop myself.

"We aren't right for each other. This life. I can't be a part of it."

"You've been in this life. You worked with your dad. He dragged you into it. Not me. It's too late to back out now. You're in it. You're compromised."

"When everything dies down…" I try to make him see reason.

"No. It won't die down. Not enough to let you go back to your old life. I'm sorry. But no. Ramirez knows who you are.

91

He's probably told his entire network of men. Even if we end him, and kill his army, you still pissed off the Irish and the Russians with the stunt your dad and you pulled." I slump back into the bed. I shouldn't have brought this up. I don't have the energy to argue with him. "You're staying here." He gets up and heads to the end of the bed.

"You can't keep me as a prisoner Massimo!" I raise my voice at him.

He turns, the glint of the beast that everyone fears rising to the surface. "Like hell I can't! You are mine. My woman. You will do as I say. You will stay where I can protect you."

"Mass, come on…"

"Enough!" He crouches down at the end of the bed. I hear the clanging of metal on metal. When he rises, he has a chain in his hand. No, no, no. He wouldn't.

"Don't do it." I try pleading with him as I try to shift away from him. With the IV tugging on one arm, and the other in a sling, I'm making little to no progress. When he reaches for my foot, I kick out at him. He grabs my leg mid-kick. In a flash, he has the shackle clasp around my ankle. I continue to thrash, to pull on the chain. It doesn't have much slack. Tears rise in my eyes. My voice is low and raspy. "I'll never forgive you for this."

The anger has faded from him. His beast calmed for now. "Yes you will. You and I will be spending a lot of time together. I will show you the kind of man I can be. How good I can be to you."

"A good man would let me go."

"I didn't say I was a good man." He's closer again. His hands reaching out to cup my cheeks. His thumbs rubbing circles and sending chills down my body. "I said I'd be good. You will want for nothing. I will provide everything you need."

His forehead leans against mine as I whisper. "Except my freedom."

"Are any of us really free?" He places a kiss on my lips. I try not to return it. I keep them immobile. He continues to move his against mine. Licking the seam of my lips. The memory of our previous kiss floods my mind. New and old sensations take over. I open without protest. His tongue immediately darts into my mouth. I'm a goner. The fight in me has left. I lean into the kiss. My mouth moving in time to his. Then he pulls back. The smile I love so much playing on his lips. "Be a good girl, and you'll have more freedom."

CHAPTER TWELVE

Massimo

The door to the study slams open and hits the wall. "You're keeping my daughter prisoner?" Shouts Raphael.

Fuck. I forgot about her fucking father.

"Yes." I admit.

Luca raises an eyebrow at me. He knows she's in my room. I haven't told him that it's involuntary. Raphael stops in his tracks. He must not have expected me to admit it. Why? I have nothing to hide.

"Let her go." He growls.

"No." I turn my back to him and continue to look at the collection of documents that Val has pulled on Ramirez. The fucker is still in hiding. It's been over a week since he escaped. For all we know he could be out of the city, hell he could no longer be in the country.

"Mass…" Luca starts. I know he's trying to look out for me. But this has nothing to do with the family. This is between me and my woman. I don't need to answer to him on this.

"No. She is mine to protect." I rebut.

Raphael joins us at the round table. He pays no attention to the work we are doing. His only concern is his daughter in the moment. I can appreciate that. Even if it does piss me off. "She's my daughter."

"And she's in this situation because of you." I spit back at him. I'm standing now and rounding the table. He takes a step back before remembering he should stand his ground. Good he has a backbone. I would hate to think one of our top enforcers is a weak pussy who won't fight for his daughter. Not that he will win. Not when it is against me.

"You have her chained to your bed." He's been in my room? That thought enrages me. No one goes in my room. I have nothing to hide. It's scarcely furnished, but it's mine.

I sense the frustration rolling off of Luca. He clearly doesn't agree with my methods but isn't saying anything. Smart man. I'm sure the idea of having a woman chained to my bed and not in the act of performing a carnal activity is enraging to him. If he were to say something, I would counter that I have seen him handcuff Elena to him a half a dozen times. The only reason I haven't done that with Livianna is because she is still healing.

"I am protecting her. She wants to run away. She doesn't understand the danger you put her in."

"She knows how to protect herself."

"From three families and a street gang? Come on Raphael, you cannot be this stupid. You set your daughter up. You put her on everyone's radar. She embarrassed countless men, learned secrets she had no business knowing, and you beat them to hell during your interrogations. Those offenses are punishable by war. Do you understand? You could have caused us all to go to war?"

"We were only discovered after your whore, Rachel,

stormed the compound and freed Ramirez. So who's really at fault here?"

My fists clench. I can feel my body shaking with the desire to punch him. To rain my fist down on him until he can no longer raise his voice to me.

Thankfully I am stopped by Luca. He grabs my shoulder and pushes me to step back. Hurting Livianna's father would just cause a bigger headache for me. She is being stubborn. Still resisting my efforts. I'm not giving up though. She'll be staying with me until she forgives me, until she falls in love with me, and then I'll put my baby in her belly and a ring on her finger so she can't leave me. Ever.

"Massimo is right Raphael. You started this. You put your daughter out there knowing there would be consequences." Luca reprimands him. Then he turns on me. "Him being wrong, doesn't make you innocent Mass. None of us saw Rachel being a decoy. You didn't spill any secrets to her, and her getting into the compound was the fault of the guards. They should know better." I smile. They do now. My fists made the message very clear. "But you did kidnap Livianna from a popular bar. People saw you walk out with her, and she hasn't been seen since. And now you are holding her prisoner, again."

"I'm keeping her safe. She's smart. She'd find a way to leave." I retort. Why can't he see my reasoning? He knows me. I am not cruel to women. Especially not my woman. Well, to be fair, I've never claimed a woman before.

"Then give her a reason to stay." He replies calmly.

Fucker. "I'm trying. You don't think I want her to choose me? To love me back?"

Raphael and Luca's jaws both drop at the same time. They speak at the same time too. "You love her?"

"Yes. I love her. I'm going to marry her." I see Raphael

start to open his mouth. "I'm not asking permission. When the time comes, when she's ready. She is getting my ring." He closes his mouth and nods.

Then he sighs. "Fuck. Do not break her heart. Do you hear me? She's my baby girl. The only thing I have left."

"I know what it's like to lose someone you love. Trust me. I won't do that to her. I'd rather rip out my own heart." Raphael nods, shakes my hand and leaves.

"You have a heart?" Laughs Luca. "When the fuck did that happen?"

I give a little chuckle. "When that woman ripped the gun from my hand and kneed me in the balls."

Luca howls with laughter. "Shit. She got you too? I thought it was just my woman."

"You better keep your women away from mine when I meet her. Don't need her getting any funny ideas." Laughs Val as he joins us at the table.

Fuck when did he get here?

Luca laughs and replies. "No promises. Knowing Elena, she'll just kick you in the balls herself." Yeah, I don't doubt she would.

When our laughter dies down, we go back to work.

"What do we know?" Asks Luca.

CHAPTER THIRTEEN

Livianna

Three weeks. That's how long I've been stuck at the compound.

Massimo took off the ankle shackle after a week, but he kept me locked in his room. At least he allowed me visitors. Yay me. Once a day my father would come to visit. I barely said two words to him. Being alone in a single room hadn't been good for my mental health and I think Massimo is finally realizing it. The quiet gave me time to think. To get lost in my mind. Nothing good came of it.

I'm angrier than I have ever been. I'm mad at Massimo for keeping me locked up. I'm mad at my Dad for taking things too far with the missions and getting me caught. I'm mad at mom for not being here. And I'm mad at myself for not seeing this coming. There were so many signs I missed. The thoughts keep me at a perpetual level of anger.

Today Massimo is taking me to see Greta and Ricco. He wants me to spend time with them. Wants us to all get to know each other. I think he's hoping I will bond with them and it will give me a reason to stay. I'm not mad at either one of them. At least not yet.

They had nothing to do with my missions, my kidnapping, or my current captivity. It's smart of Massimo. I won't tell him that. I've been keeping my thoughts on him and his efforts to myself. Why? Because he's tearing down my walls. He's showering me with affection and even though I'm still angry, I want so badly to lap it all up. To roll around in it and tell him all is forgiven and to take me to bed so we can have that elusive make-up sex Ashley talked about.

Speaking of Ashley. Luca let's me call and text her now. I want to go see her. He has refused to let me. He did finally concede that she could come to the Compound. I told him no. She doesn't know about my connection. Not yet. I don't want her coming when we are in the middle of a potential massive war.

The ring of the doorbell has me refocusing on the task at hand. I'm nervous. And I hate that I am. It feels like I'm meeting the parents of a boyfriend for the first time. I guess in a sense I am. A very twisted and warped sense. Massimo says I'm his, which I guess is the equivalent of girlfriend in his eyes. Like I said, warped. And Ricco and Greta filled a parental roll in Massimo's life as a teen. So they are the parents in this twisted scenario.

Massimo's mom isn't in the picture, and he doesn't like to talk about his dad, Giuseppe. Ricco and him were best friends growing up, and raised their boys together until shit hit the fan in Giuseppe's marriage. Ricco has continued to be there for him as much as he can, but the relationship has never been the same.

A beautiful, short red headed woman with a flour covered baking apron on answers the door. "You're here! Finally!" I expect her to be talking about Massimo, but she flings herself at me. Her arms wrap around me and hug me tight. It's warm and comforting. Just like a mother's should be.

Shit. I feel the prickle of tears itching at my eyes. Nope. Not happening. Not crying right now. I blink a few times until the feeling recedes. I give her a hug in return. "I'm guessing you're Greta." I feel her belly and chest shake with a laugh before she pulls back.

Her hands pinch at my cheeks as she looks deep into my eyes. "I am. And you are Massimo's Livianna."

"I'm not…" It's become habit to attempt to correct everyone. Usually it is Massimo who stops me. With either a pinch to the hip, a boop on the nose, or a kiss on the lips. Today it is none of the above.

Greta is the one to stop me. "Nonsense. He's claimed you. To the Caruso men, that is as good as a marriage contract."

"A what!" My eyes flick from Greta to Massimo and back. Looking for any sign, any hint of a joke, a lie, something.

I see nothing.

Ricco joins us at the door. Coming up behind Greta, and pulling her back into his arms. Her back leaning against his chest. Her shoulder falling back to rest on him. She looks so happy, content. "It's true. When we claim a woman it's for life. I claimed my Greta. Gio claimed Helen." I sense Massimo tense at the mention of his parents. There is a story there. One I want to know, but won't push for. Yet. "Bosco claimed Violet, Luca claimed Elena, and now Massimo here has claimed you." Explains Ricco.

Massimo is nodding his head along. His arms crossed over his chest as though to say I dare you to argue. I don't. I'm beginning to understand. I think a piece of me always understood.

Massimo must sense my resolve breaking. He pulls me into his arms and kisses me on the forehead. "Come. Let's go inside. Elena and Luca will be here soon."

I nod my head and allow him to pull me into the house. It is beautifully decorated. Lots of vibrant and warm colors intermixed throughout the house. They don't look like that should go together, but somehow Greta pulled it off.

An hour later, Elena, Luca, Val, and Milan have joined us. I have gotten to know Milan a bit more. Turns out she and I are a lot alike. Both faking parts of our personality to hide our true selfs. While mine was a chosen facade to bear. Milan's was forced on her. Her mother had been trying to groom her into a perfect Mafia bride for Luca. Or rather, her version of a Mafia bride.

From a young age, Milan was taught to apply make-up, walk in six inch heels, and wear tight and revealing clothing. Turns out, all the mother's torturous beauty routines were for nothing. Milan's contract became void when Elena showed up. She's once again free to choose who she wishes to marry.

She's also free to dress and act as she wishes. Gone are the dresses and heels. She wears them on occasion but the heel is lower, and the dresses longer and less revealing. Her make-up is now minimal and instead of pouring over fashion magazines, Milan has taken up reading about chemistry and physics. She's a real bookworm.

Most importantly. She looks happy.

Milan never used to be included in these get together's between Luca, Massimo and Val. She was an outsider. Much like how I feel now. Her mother's influence caused the guys to shun Milan. They didn't want to be involved in the drama. Now they happily include her when they can. She is still young. Only fifteen. She's sweet. I like her. And so does everyone else, now.

"So, Massimo, are you going to see your father tonight?" Asks Ricco.

"No." Massimo replies.

Ricco continues to look right at him, though Massimo ignores his stare. "It's Thursday." Ricco adds.

"It is." Massimo answers the non-question evasively.

"You always see him on Thursdays." Chimes in Greta.

Massimo tenses beside me. He's been keeping me close all afternoon. I don't think it's because he thinks I'll try to sneak away. I have better sense than that. I think he needs me. Needs my comfort even though I haven't freely given it thus far.

"Not tonight." Massimo's voice is getting sharper.

I turn to him. My hip bumping into his. "We can go see him if you want."

His eyes soften a bit, but his words are still harsh. "No."

The anger in me builds. What has been the point of this then? He wants me to get to know the people in his life, yet he doesn't want me to meet the one that should be the most important. "Yes." I counter with my own anger laced in the word.

Without breaking eyes contact, Massimo addresses the room. "Leave us." One by one, everyone stands and exits. Luca and Elena are the last to leave.

"Tell her. She needs to know." Says Luca.

Elena puts her hand on Massimo's shoulder. "You were the one who said you want her to know you. This is knowing you. The good, the bad, all of it." Elena then turns to face me. I wouldn't say we are friends. Not yet. I could see it happening someday. Maybe. "You said you trust her. Show her you mean it."

Then she turns, accepts Luca's offered hand and vanishes

around the corner.

Suddenly I'm lifted into the air, and plopped onto Massimo's lap. I'm straddling his thighs. My mind flashes to the night he stripped off my clothes.

I can't think about that now.

"Need to hold you." He grumbles as he pulls me in tight. His face is buried in my hair. I let him hold me. He has done this a lot over the last few weeks. At first I always protested it. I didn't want him to touch me. Now I crave it. I like feeling the evidence of his desire pressed against my thigh. "My dad's an alcoholic."

I use my arms to pull Massimo's face out of my hair. I gently cup his jaw. It's a move he's done several times to me. I find it comforting. I'm hoping he does too.

"It's a long story. I'll tell you the whole thing someday, but basically we were poor. My dad worked a lot to try to change that. Mom was unhappy. She cheated on my dad. When he found out he wanted to work things out. She didn't. She ran off with the guy she was seeing. We haven't seen her since. Dad loved her. Her leaving broke him. Hasn't been the same since."

"I'm so sorry Massimo." I lean my forehead against his the way he likes.

"After that, I had trouble trusting people. And I don't give second chances. I don't like cheaters, liars, or manipulators. It's why I'm keeping you close. I can't stand the thought of you with another guy. I wasn't lying when I said I want you safe. Need you safe. It's more than that. You're gorgeous. Beautiful. It wouldn't be hard for someone to steal you from me."

"Yes it would." His eyes grow big at my admission.

"No it wouldn't." He counters. His shoulders slumping.

I dig my fingers into his cheeks harder. Then slam my

lips into his for a punishing kiss. I want that thought out of his head. He takes a moment to respond. When he does, he is putting every cell of his body into that kiss. I have to break away after a few minutes to catch my breathe. I was on the verge of passing out from oxygen deprivation.

"Yes it would." My hands are still on his face. My eyes locked on his. "I love you Massimo." His grip on me tightens and I swear I feel his already large and hard erection grow even more. "You're stubborn and a pain in my ass most of the time. But I love you. No one will take me away from you."

"But the other guys…" He still doesn't understand what I did on those missions. I tap my pointed finger on his nose. "Did you just boop me?" He asks with a laugh.

"I did." I reply with a smile. "Massimo, I never slept with any of those guys. Never took off my clothes. I kissed one. I didn't want it, and I hated it. You're the only one I want. The only one I have ever wanted, and the only one I will want."

He looks only half convinced. I suck in a deep breath. Preparing myself to share my final secret with him. "I'm a virgin."

I think he stops breathing. He is frozen in my arms.

"Massimo?"

He doesn't respond.

"Honey?"

He sucks in a breath. His eyes blink away the far away look they had taken on.

"I was waiting for the right person. One I too could trust. I trust you Massimo. I love you. I only want you."

"I want you too. Only you. I'll never cheat on you, I swear. I'll never touch another woman." That brings a smile to my face and warmth to my heart.

"Good." I wrap my arms tighter around him, and bury my head in the spot between his shoulder and neck. It's where his cologne and natural scent is strongest. My Massimo. He claimed me. Now I'm claiming him.

"Fuck yes!" Shouts Val from the doorway.

Massimo and I turn at the same time. Everyone is gathered there. Including one new person. A slightly disheveled, red eyed older man. I look to Massimo, then back at him. The similarities are hard not to notice. This must be his father.

I quickly extract myself from Massimo's arms and stand. Then I reach for Massimo to help him stand. Not that he needs it. If he did, I'm sure I wouldn't be able to make him budge. He is solid muscle. And I love it.

"Dad?" Asks Massimo. It's like he can't believe he's here.

"Your mother called." His dad replies. Massimo stiffens.

"What did she want?" I tuck myself under Massimo's arm and latch onto his waist. I'm hoping my presence lends him a bit of strength.

"Her husband ran off with his secretary. Wants to know if she can come stay with me for a bit until she's back on her feet." Massimo growls next to me and takes a step towards his dad, who holds up his hands in a gesture of compliance and innocence. "I told her to fuck off. Told her she's on her own." He exhales loudly. A few tears drip down his cheeks.

I use my hand on Massimo's lower back to push him forward. He needs it literally and mentally. Whether he wants to admit it or not, his dad and him need each other right now.

"She said she's sorry. She misses us. And she still loves us." His dad breaks. His knees buckle. Massimo is there to catch him. Milan, Val and Elena are the first to leave. They each give Massimo a smile and nod. Letting him know they are here for him. But leaving so as to not intrude on a family matter.

Greta and Luca leave next.

Ricco is beside his friend. Rubbing his back. Offering him his silent comfort.

"For the first time in years, I felt nothing. I had been waiting so long for her to come back, and now I don't want her. I don't want to drink." He looks up at Massimo. "I want help. I need help. I should never have abandoned you." He holds a hand against Massimo's cheek.

Massimo covers his dad's hand in his own. He presses it harder against him as Massimo leans into it. I'm willing to bet this is the first time in years they have held each other or shown this level of affection.

"You didn't abandon me." Massimo says. His eyes starting to glisten.

"I did." Gio sobs.

Massimo grabs his father's face. He holds him steady, ensuring their eyes remain locked. "No. You didn't. You were still here. If I needed you, I know you would have been there. Drunk or not. I know it was hard for you. You loved mom." His dad nods his head in Massimo's hands. Not breaking eye contact. "And the days I visited. You didn't drink until I left. You know I needed that, even though you needed that drink."

His dad nods again, eye contact breaking as he closes his eyes and sobs harder. Massimo grabs his dad by the back of his neck and smashes him into him. Chest to chest, they cling to each other.

Ricco and I let them have their moment. Knowing they both need this. Both need to let go of the past.

"I want to go to rehab. I need it." Pleads Gio. "I don't want to drink anymore. I don't need it. When your mother called, I realized I didn't love her anymore. Not like I did. I got the closure I didn't want to admit I needed."

Massimo nods. "I'll take you dad."

"No." Gio pulls back slightly so he can look at his son. "I already asked Ricco and Greta to drop me off. I have already booked my room for ninety days. I came to apologize, and to meet your girl." They break away from their hug and Massimo calls me over with a silent nod of his head.

"Hi Mr. D'Angelo." I greet him.

Massimo tucks me under his arm again. "Please, call me Gio." He says as he takes my hand and gives a little shake before bringing my knuckles up to his lips for a gentle kiss. "Take care of my boy for me."

The tears I was trying to hold back fall. "I will." I say with a sniffle. "You take care of yourself. And call us often."

His face lights up at that. "I will, sweetheart. I'll need to get to know my daughter-in-law before the wedding."

Massimo tenses next to me. Surprisingly I don't. Any fear I might have had about marry Massimo seems to have faded when I told him I loved him. When I declared him mine. I'm not ready to marry yet. We have to still deal with Ramirez first.

I grip tighter to Massimo. "Sounds good."

CHAPTER FOURTEEN

Massimo

I used to love coming to Club Vivid with Luca. It's a Caruso establishment and we have the entire VIP section to ourselves. Tonight, I hate it. I may never come back. Girls from the past are eying me like a piece of meat.

In the past I might have soaked up the attention and taken one of their girlfriends to a hotel to bang. Presently, I am trying to keep their hands off of me, while I dance with my girl. We could have danced in VIP, but no. She wanted the real Vivid experience. I bet it was Elena's idea. She's a shit-stirrer. It's why Luca has her handcuffed to him upstairs. He won't let her down here again after last time.

Livianna spins in my arms. Her hips swaying to the beat, her legs straddling my thigh. Another inch closer and she could rub herself to orgasm on my leg. Fuck. Why is that image getting me hard?

Because I have had a perpetual boner since meeting Liv and my fist in the shower is just not doing it for me anymore. I'm trying to be patient. Liv confessed she's a virgin and I want to make her first time special. Problem is, we're too fucking busy. War is closing in on us. The Russians want answers, the Irish attacked our docks, and Ramirez is still missing.

Liv says that our last rat, Joseph, the one who hasn't been seen since the night I kidnapped her will have answers, and he doesn't have the money or the clout in another organization to run. He's still somewhere in the city.

Val and Elena have been pouring over cameras throughout the city looking for him. They set up alerts if his credit cards or bank account are accessed. Luca spoke to the police chief about putting a BOLO out for him.

We'll find him. It's only a matter of time.

Meanwhile, Elena and Livianna convinced us we needed to take a night off. I think they were sick of our piss poor moods. Liv was also sick of seeing me come back to the room with blood on my shirt and hands. She's been understanding. She knows this is who I am, and that I'm taking every precaution to be safe while doing it so I get back home to her.

If I had had it my way, I would have forgone the club, and instead done a romantic evening in with my girl. I've got champagne, flowers, and candles ready to be lit in our room. Milan helped set it up. The girl is a true romantic.

Not going to lie. I used to despise her. I thought she was just like her mother. A manipulative bitch. I was wrong. We all were. She isn't anything like her mother. To keep the peace and her mother happy over the years, she played the roll well. As soon as Ravinia was out of the Compound, and away from Milan, her true character has come out.

Turns out, she is smart, sweet, loyal, and loving. She admitted she was upset to learn Luca was taking Elena as his bride and not her, but she understood. Even said Elena was a better match for him anyway. Now Elena and Milan are making huge strides in their sisterly bonding. Val and Luca are getting in on it too, so I threw my hat in.

I'm glad I did. Milan helped me to come up with a plan for tonight. I'm supposed to text her when we leave the club. She'll have everything set up when we get back to the Compound. The flower petals will be in a heart shape on the bed, candles lit around the room and in the bathroom, and a hot bath will be drawn with lavender oil and more petals floating in the water with the bubbles.

It's not something I could have come up with on my own, so I'm thankful to have her help. I think Livianna's going to love it. I'm hoping tonight we can take the next step in our relationship. If she's not ready tonight, I won't pressure her. I'll spoil her. I can still bathe her and sip champagne as we talk and snuggle on the couch.

Snuggle?

Who the fuck have I become?

A hand that is not my girl's grabs my ass and squeezes. My ass cheeks clench hard. "Enough of this." I bark out. Livianna looks around me to the woman who touched me.

"Don't touch what's mine!" Her growl is dark and menacing. I wasn't sure my girl had it in her, but fuck if it isn't the hottest thing I've ever heard.

"We're leaving." I say. Then bend, put my should in her stomach, and lift. Her upper body falls forward over my shoulder.

"Massimo!" She flails in my arms.

Not wanting to drop her, I smack her on each cheek in rapid succession. "Did you just…" She trails off as I smack her left cheek again.

"Yes I did. Now shush. We're going upstairs. You can keep dancing if you want, but it will be for me. Only me. Got it?"

She is silent for a moment, until I smack her again. "Okay, okay, I got it."

The smile remains on my face as I climb the stairs to the third floor. It's the one above VIP. My office is up here. Or at least one of them. I have a few scattered around town. It used to be my go to. I could stand looking out the one way mirror down at the club and pick out the girl I was going to fuck that night. Sometimes I would point out a girl to one of my men and they would go and fetch her for me. They'd bring her up where I'd let them give me a blowjob or I'd bang them over the desk before sending them away.

I was an asshole. I'll admit it.

I lower Livianna to her feet after I get her inside and lock and close the door. She's free to leave if she wants. I'm done making her my prisoner. She is free to leave at anytime. But my girl no longer wants to leave. She wants me.

Looking around the room, I'm glad I had all the furniture replaced and the entire room deep cleaned. I didn't want to bring Livianna up here to reenact the past. I brought her up here so I can make new memories here. I changed the room so it was as close to a new room as possible that I could make without demolishing the club.

Knowing how much my girl's mind picks up the details, I'm sure she has already noticed the new furniture smell. She moves to the desk, her back to me, her finger running over the dark wood. "New?" She asks.

I smile and nod.

"Good."

"I didn't bring you up here to fuck you on my new desk." She look surprised. "You didn't."

"No. I can if you want me to." I say as I close the distance between us and take her lips into mine. "I just couldn't stand sharing you for a moment longer." I say as I pull back. Liv leans with me. Chasing my lips.

"I didn't like sharing you either." She leans her head against my chest. "Is it always like that? Are you always touched and grabbed?"

I nod. "Yeah. I didn't use to say no. I let anyone touch me, and I touched anyone I wanted." I put a finger under her chin and lift her head. "That's not me anymore. I didn't get aroused by them downstairs." I take one of her hands and run it along my hard length. "This is all you. Their touch made my skin crawl. I kept trying to get them away."

"I saw. You looked awfully uncomfortable." She says with a giggle.

I boop her on the nose. She's too cute when she giggles like that.

Cute? Holy shit. Do I still have my man card? I want to check if I still have my balls, but I don't want to ruin the moment. Besides, if I lost them to her, I'll be okay. They are safe with her. All of me is.

I grab her by the hips and walk her backwards towards the window. Her shoulders touch glass first. Then my mouth is on hers. I breathe her in like she's my lifeline to this world. Like she's the tether to my soul. It's hard to remember my life before her when she is in my arms.

When I've gotten my fill of her lips, I spin her around. Her hands slap against the window to brace herself. My lips move down her neck. Sucking. Biting. Needing to make my mark so everyone knows she is mine.

"Massimo." My name comes out like a whisper. I take it as encouragement. One hand glides up to squeeze her breast, the other slides down to the hem of her skirt. I hook my fingers under the fabric and pull it up as I slide my hand closer to her center. I can feel the heat coming off her. I swear I can smell her arousal from here. I have to know. Reaching out a finger, I brush against her pantie covered pussy.

"Fuck, sweetheart. You're drenched." I growl into her hair. Forgetting her breasts, I wrap my one hand in her hair and yank her head back. I need her mouth.

Lips collide and our tongues duel against one another. This is no winner. We don't need one. My tongue just wants to play with her. My whole body does.

I release her lips and hair. Returning my focus to her breasts and slit. I tease my fingers into her panties and slide along the pooling wetness. A groan of appreciation escapes me. I can't and won't stop the noises. Hers either. I want her loud. I want everyone to hear how much I satisfy my woman.

"Massimo." Her voice is more urgent.

"I got you babe. Let me take care of you." I murmur.

"No." She replies. That halts me in my tracks.

"What's wrong?" I remove my hands from her body even though it pains me to do so. I like touching her, but I'll stop if I'm making her uncomfortable.

"Not you." She says with reassuring eyes, and a caressing touch to my cheek. I let out the breathe I was holding, cause fuck me. If I can't kiss and touch her I'm in for a long lifetime of solo handjobs. "Look."

I move to the window and follow her finger. Those two men. At the end of the bar. Blue button up and black sweater."

"I see them." I reply. Not sure who they are but I see them.

"They are going to drug that woman." She says moving her finger to a woman in a dark green dress."

"How do you know?" I can't see any indicators in their posture or mannerisms like she can.

"Look at the one in blue's left hand. See how it looks like it's clenched into a fist. He's holding the drugs. He holds it in his non-dominate hand, so he can approach the girl and use his right hand to greet her. He's going to appear like a gentleman to get her to trust him. He'll appear different than the sleazy guys who go straight for the corny pick-ups lines."

I watch as what she says happens exactly like she said it would. Holy shit! They are kidnapping girls from our club. Fuck that. Not on my watch.

I turn to alert our guards. They are stationed at every door.

"Wait." She says and takes my hand. "We need to wait until we know who the third guy is."

"How do you know there is a third?"

"It's their M.O." She replies. "I've been watching them during my missions. At first I didn't realize what I was seeing. Then it hit me, and it's how I messed up Ramirez' last shipment. I noticed a trend of three guys drugging a girl then appearing to be a doting boyfriend and friends taking the girl home when she was drunk. The drug doesn't knock you out completely. It makes your muscles slack. So you slur your words and stumble if you try to walk. It seriously looks like you're just drunk. It looks so real and they play their part so well that the bodyguards don't question it. They let them walk out the front door."

"Not today." I say. "Let's get down there."

Together we descend the steps. Along the way I shoot off a text to Luca, Val, and our team of guards. They will notify the club security. Livianna grabs my hand when we reach the dance-floor. She whispers to me to follow her lead. I do. Hand in hand, she leads me in a half dance, half march to get closer to the girl. When she is within a few feet. Liv stops.

"Black shirt, gray pants. Quarter inch beard at your nine o'clock." Nothing about those words should have been sexy. None of them should have my cock twitch. I can't wait to get her home later so I can worship her body. "We've got about fifteen seconds before she feels the drugs. She'll stumble and one of the guys will grab her, and pretend to steady her. Then his friend will come over, appearing to help. Third guy will grab her coat. Then they will head to the door. We need to let them."

"What?" She can't be serious.

"We need to know where they are taking the girls. The last warehouse was burned to the ground. Once I found it, they weren't going to bring their next shipment there. We need to find out their new location, and we need to try and save anyone already there, and take care of the rest of the scum stealing and selling them."

"You're right." Fuck my girl is smart and crafty. We'll need to talk more about her messing with the last shipment. I'm willing to bet she put herself into danger to do it, and I won't tolerate her doing that again. Her safety is top priority.

Sure enough, fifteen seconds have passed and the girl stumbles on her feet. Blue shirt grabs her, black sweater comes to help and gray pants grabs her coat. If I hadn't been watching them, I absolutely would have thought nothing more of a drunk girl getting helped home by her boyfriend.

I grab Liv's hand and pull her along to the back door. There are three SUVs waiting for us in the alley. Luca and Elena in one with guards, Val and his guards in another, and Livianna and I bringing up the rear.

We work as a team keeping them off our scent as we tail them. We have one car at a safe distance behind them while the other two loop a nearby block. Then the tail car splits off and one of the others takes its place. We repeat this play until we near the shipyard. Fuck. They are keeping them at the docks. It's a smaller port than the one we control.

We give the men we are following a few minutes before

Luca calls to strike.

"Stay here." I tell Livianna as I pull my gun out and open the door.

"Seriously? You wouldn't even be here without me." I press a kiss to her lips.

"I know. You're amazing. But I won't risk you getting hurt. We have enough men to take care of this. You stay here."

"Mass…" She begins to grumble but I cut her off.

"For me. Do this for me." Her arms cross over her chest and she leans back into her seat.

"Fine. Hurry back."

I smile at my girl and nod before running to catch up with Luca and the men.

There are more men than we predicted. Bullets are spraying everywhere. Crates of unknown product are being ripped apart. The men we are attacking aren't good shots. They seem to be shooting at an area and not a person. It's a waste of bullets.

We didn't have time to circle around the building and secure all the exits. Luca decided to move fast. Hoping to take them off guard enough to take them down before they could run.

Hope wasn't enough. There are men fleeing the back door. A second wave of gunfire is happening. This one beyond that door. Is there a third party here? Who are they attacking, or being attacked by.

Luca and I each drop one last man. The room goes quiet. A few more shots ring out outside. I take off running without another thought. I stop before the door and look out the window. I stay mostly hidden to avoid being shot at.

It only takes a second for my eyes to land on her. Livianna. She's still in the car. But the car isn't around front.

116

Sneaky girl.

Luca and I run outside. Val and Al hot on our trail. Before I can get to her, another car is ramming it into Liv's driver door. "NO!" I scream. My legs carry me as fast as I can across the lot. I'm nearly too late. The driver of the other car gets out, gun in his hand. He rips Liv's door open. She is lumped against the wheel. A gash on her forehead and the start of a bruise on her cheek. It looks like she beings to stir when the man grabs her and drags her from the car. He gets her on her feet, then slams the butt of the gun down on her head. She collapses to the ground right before I tackle the dead bastard.

I pound my fists into his face over and over. I hear the crunching of bones. Still I continue to pummel his face.

I feel a hand on my shoulder. I shrug it off and hit the now unrecognizable man again. "Mass, enough. He's dead."

My first pauses mid-air. He's right. The fucker isn't breathing. His nose has been ground to fragments, and their is brain matter seeping out of his broken skull.

"Liv needs you." Says Luca. That does it. I snap out of whatever trance I was in.

I crawl over to her. She is awake. Barely. "I'm so sorry sweetheart." I pull her into my arms and rock us back and forth.

The rest of our men surround us. There is a group of about fifteen woman huddled by the back hatch of one of the SUVs. Our field medics are looking them over and addressing the injuries we can. Luca is calling for transport and the staff at the hospital we own under the Caruso name are being prepped to take us in.

Val is helping their latest victim, the girl in the blue dress sip water. The drug is already leaving her system.

A series of screeching tires has us all tensing and drawing our weapons. Even my Liv, whose practically asleep in my arms pulls out her gun from her purse. I would laugh if I wasn't so concerned with our new visitors.

"Where is she?" Growls a man in a fresh pressed suit from the third car.

"Who are you?" Asks Luca as he steps to the front. Elena is at his side, her gun pointed at the man in the suit.

The man in the suit stops walking. His eyes flicker around to each of us, then to the bodies scattered about. "Looks like you had a hell of a party." He takes a step closer to one of the fallen. He gives him a kick with his foot until the body rolls to reveal the face. "Cartel?" He asks, looking back at Luca.

"Yeah, and you are?" Asks Luca again.

The man returns to walking towards Luca. He stops a few feet from him and extends his arm. "Ivan. Ivan Vasiliev."

"Russian." Grumbles Luca. He takes his hand in his and shakes it. It's a peace offering for the moment. It means we can all lower our weapons which we do.

"What happened here?" Questions Ivan.

"Three fuckers thought they could kidnap a girl from our club. We don't allow that shit. Decided we could knock more of their operation if we let them lead us to their warehouse. We were right. Found fifteen other girls, and put down twelve guards. There's still one alive. Plan on torturing him to see what else he knows." Answers Luca. Then he crosses his arms over his chest. "What are you doing here?"

Ivan scrubs a hand down his face. Looks like he's having as long of a night as we are. "My fucking sister snuck off. Ditched her guard. I've got a tracker on her. It pinged here before going dead."

"All the girls we found are over there." Says Luca as he nods to the gathering of girls. "Except for the one taken tonight. She's still a little woozy from the drugs in her system. My brother Val is trying to get her to drink some water to help."

"Lena!" Barks Ivan. His eyes set on the girl in Val's arms. He's not touching her inappropriately. His arm is around her waist, but high enough not to skim her butt. His jacket is draped over her shoulders and hiding her low cut neckline.

Ivan stomps over to her. Giving Val a nod of appreciate as he takes her from him. He carries her over to his SUV. "Viktor was fucking worried sick about you. Don't you ever pull this shit again. You hear me?"

I'm not sure she does. She's pretty out of it still.

Ivan returns to Luca. "I owe you a debt. You saved my sister, and three of the girls you saved are ones we've been looking for." Luca nods in return. Debts are powerful chips to cash in in our world. "I'll be taking over the Russian territory soon. Mishkin is dangerous, unpredictable. I could use an Allie when I take over."

Luca thinks it over for a moment. Then turns to me. I know what he is thinking. We want the Cartel gone, he wants the Russian throne. It's a good deal all around, plus it earns us a powerful new Allie.

"You help us end this skin trade and exterminate the Cartel from Chicago, we'll help you with your coupe." Luca holds out his hand for Ivan to shake.

"Seal it with blood?" Asks Ivan.

Fuck. He means a marriage contract. A union between our two families.

This time Luca doesn't look at me. I know what he's thinking. It's got to be either Val or Milan. There is no one else high enough in our organization. Well, there is me. I'm not technically married, yet, but I'll be damned if anyone takes away my Livianna.

"I've got a brother of marrying age now. Or a sister of my

wife not recognized by blood but by the Council as my predecessors second daughter. She's fifteen."

Ivan turns to who we can assume is his second in command. They whisper for a brief moment before Ivan answers. "I have no other sisters, and Lena is taken. My Second has a sister who's eight. Your Val can either marry her, or I can marry the second sister."

Luca looks to Val. He gives a noncommittal shrug. He's currently unattached, but ten years is a long time to wait to solidify an alliance. "Would you be faithful to a wife, or would you expect to be allowed a mistress?"

"I have no time for mistresses." Replies Ivan.

"That's not an answer." Pipes in Elena.

Instead of being mad, Ivan looks pleased. "You must be Elena. The first daughter. The unknown heir." Fuck. He's done his homework.

"I am. And you still didn't answer the question. Would you be faithful to Milan?"

"I would." He takes a momentary pause. "I cannot promise we will love each other. Best I can offer is that I will be a respectable life companion. There will be needs she will be expected to meet. I will not force myself on her, and I would need an heir."

Luca answers quickly. "I wish to get Milan's approval, if it's alright with you. If she does not accept, Val will marry your second's sister."

"I look forward to hearing from you," Ivan replies and offers his hand to shake on it.

CHAPTER FIFTEEN

Livianna

We ended up spending the night at the hospital. I needed a few stitches, and Massimo demanded I be monitored overnight due to my mild concussion. I thought it was unnecessary, but I didn't dare tell him that. He was on edge. My being injured nearly sent him into a tailspin, so I let him call the shots and fuss over me.

He left me only a couple of times and didn't go any further than into the hallway. Luca and Val were coordinating the care of the girls we found. Ivan had even followed us with his team so his sister could get looked at. At one point there was a loud commotion a few rooms down from me. Apparently her fiancé had arrived and gone ballistic when he heard what happened.

Their story sounds similar to Elena and Luca's. Ivan arranged a marriage for his sister to marry Viktor, the first son of the Detroit Pakhan in exchange for support when he stages his coupe to take the Chicago throne from Mishkin. Apparently it was love at first sight for Viktor. Not so much

Lena. She's been giving him a hard time.

I heard Elena offer up Luca's handcuffs to him. Luca had grumbled, but ended up handing them over. I laughed from my bed, wishing I could have been with them to see. Knowing Luca, I'm sure he will pay Elena back for that, and get her a collar or something permanent.

It's now early afternoon and Massimo and I are finally headed to our room. I can't wait to take a shower. Massimo had given me a sponge bath at the hospital after he refused to let any of the nurses do it.

I had no complaints. His hands lingered on my breasts a bit longer than professional. Other than that, he was a gentleman and I appreciated it. I was getting turned on by the heated look in his eyes, and as much as I was ready to take the plunge with him and give him my virginity, I did not want it on an uncomfortable hospital bed with both strangers and family only feet away in the hallway.

Massimo is ahead of me when we reach our door. He seems to pause at it for a moment before he opens the door wide. He doesn't step in. I tilt my head and give him a curious look. His answer to my nonverbal question is to nod towards the room. His lips turning up into a smile.

I give him a small smile back and enter the room. It take a moment for my brain to connect to what my eyes were seeing. When they do, the whole room clouds. My vision becoming blurry with tears.

Hundreds of roses and tulips are scattered around the room. A couple dozen flameless candles light a path to the bed, as well as split off and lead a second path to the bathroom. I move forward a few steps. Next to the bed is a bottle of champagne on ice, and two empty flutes. The bed has a new red comforter on it with white rose petals placed in the shape of a heart in the center.

I turn quickly and launch into Massimo's arms. He laughs as he catches me. "I love you Massimo."

"I love you too Livianna." His lips press mine in a tender kiss. It's perfect. This moment is perfect.

"How did you do all this?" I ask. He hasn't left my side for more than a few minutes in almost twenty-four hours.

Taking my hand, he leads me deeper into the room. He stops to fill up the glasses of champagne. Then hands me one before leading me into the bathroom. This room is decorated too. The bathtub is filled with water, bubbles, and flowers. The counters are lined with more candles. "I bought everything two days ago and kept it in a guest room down the hall. I was waiting for the right time. The plan was to surprise you last night when we got back from the Club. Milan had offered her help. She knew where everything was. As soon as I texted her we were on our way home, she rushed to get this all done."

"Thank you." I says with as much sincerity as I can muster. My heart is overflowing with the love I feel for this man.

"Let's take a bathe first. I don't think the one at the hospital should count."

"You just want to see me naked and wet." I'm surprised by the level of sass I let out.

He barks a laugh, as his large, calloused hands grasp the hem of my dress and pull it over my body and drops it on the floor. There was no way I could wear a bra with it's plunging neckline, so sanes the dress, I'm left with only a pair of panties. His hands skim up and down my sides as he takes my mouth in a long, slow kiss.

While my brain still functions, I have the mind to unbutton his shirt and shift it off his shoulders so it too can fall to the floor. He takes a step back from me and removes his undershirt.

Damn, I love looking at him. His deeply cut muscles beg for me to run my hands, or tongue on them. Later. I promise myself I will later. My hands then go to his belt. I get it undone before my hands begin to shake. I knew I would be nervous, I just didn't realize I would be this nervous. I mean, it's Massimo. The man I love. Why should I be nervous about finally making love to him? Holy shit. Is that what we are doing? Are we having sex, or are we making love?

A tap on my nose stops my train of thought. "Are you always going to boop me?"

"Are you always going to ignore me when I'm naked in favor of your secret thoughts?" I take a moment to realize what he said before my eyes scan down his body. Stopping at the rather large appendage that is standing tall and leaking from the tip.

"Holy shit." I whisper, not too quietly. He's huge.

He gives a laugh before his hand goes to his swollen cock and gives it a stroke. My eyes are mesmerized at the motion. "You can touch it." I tear my eyes from his cock to look at his eyes, but my eyes have a mind of their own, and go back down. "It's not going to bite you."

This time, I'm the one who laughs. "I know. I just…I've never." His hand under my chin, lifts my gaze to his. His lips press softly on mine.

"I know babe. Look, touch, suck. Whatever you want to do, I'm yours."

"And I'm yours." I whisper back.

"Damn right you are. Now let's ignore the big guy and get in the bath. If you want to explore more when we get done, we can. Let me take care of you first." I don't have the words so I nod and let him pull me into the bathe. The water is warm. The scent of lavender hitting my senses and immediately calming my nerves.

Massimo sinks down into the water behind me. Once he's settled he pulls my back to his front. His erection digging into my ass. I give a little squirm. Curious about the feel of it. Massimo's hands go to my hips and holds me still. "Steady sweetheart. I truly meant I was only going to wash you in here."

I can't help the moan of disappointment as it escapes my lips. Massimo doesn't sound too put off. In fact his hands reach up to tug and pinch my already pointed nipple. They are so sensitive, another moan slips out.

Massimo's mouth joins the action next with a kiss to my neck, then a bite, and then another kiss. He repeats the action until I am a moaning mess. Begging him to touch me where I need him most. He doesn't. Instead his lips and hands leave my body.

I want to argue and yell for him to put them back, until he has the hand sprayer for the water running over my head, followed by a hand massaging in shampoo. "Oh god, that feels good."

"I'll always take care of my girl." He whispers. "Here," he rubs my scalp with his left hand. "And here." His right hand is suddenly between my legs. Sliding through my slit, gliding by my entrance and then tenderly stroking my clit.

"Oh god." My back arches as he continues his ministrations. Then all too soon his hands are gone, and he is rinsing out my hair. "You're such a tease." I admonish him.

He doesn't respond with words. Just rubs conditioner through my hair before rinsing it out as well. He's quick to wash my body after that, not allowing his hands or fingers to linger anywhere too long. Once I'm washed and scrubbed from hair to toe, he quickly washes himself before draining the bath water. He stands first. His erection now looking painful. The tip is purple and the vein running along the underside looks angry.

Without thought, my hand goes up to stroke it. Feeling the harden member in mine feels right. I've never touched anyone else's cock before. And I don't want to. No one else's would feel this right. Because it's Massimo. I look up into Massimo's eyes as I stick out my tongue to taste the tip.

His eyes flair right as his essence floods my taste buds. I want more.

I don't get it. As soon as I lean in for another lick, I am picked up and thrown over his shoulder. "Your mouth is not the first hole I'm claiming sweetheart. I won't last long tonight. You've got me too worked up. I need to be inside you. Claiming you."

God, his dirty talk sends another rush of wetness from my core to my pussy. I need him too. I can't wait any longer. I feel so empty. I need him filling me up. Now.

Massimo is quick to lay me on the bed. I scoot back until I hit the pillows. He follows. Crawling towards me like a jungle cat hunting its prey. I'm not scared. The nerves are gone too. It's just me and Massimo in here. I know I have nothing to be worried about. He'll take care of me. I'm aware their will be pain initially, but I also know without a doubt that this experience will be perfect, nothing fumbled, awkward, or unsatisfying about it. It will be the best losing of virginity story there could be, but no one will hear about it. I won't be sharing this with anyone. This moment is Massimo's and mine.

Massimo is on top of me now. Allowing his weight to brush over me without crushing me. I want more. I want his touch, the weight, the pain, the pleasure. I reach up and hook my arms around his neck. "Make love to me Massimo." I murmur as I take his lips.

"I love you Livianna." He says between kisses.

"I love you too, Massimo."

"I want you to scream and moan my name. Don't hold back okay. This is all about you. You don't like something, speak up, don't endure it for me, got it." The threat of tears prickles my eyes. I can't form words. I nod instead and kiss him again.

I feel the press of his cock at my entrance. He slides the first inch in. There isn't pain. Mild discomfort as I feel my walls stretching to accommodate him. His hips roll forward and he sinks a bit deeper.

Then he stills. His eyes going between us. I follow his gaze. Fuck! Who knew the sight would be so erotic. I take that back. A lot of people do, I mean isn't that the point of porn?

"Liv." His words are soft, as his finger bops me on the nose. My eyes shoot to him, my cheeks flushing red from embarrassment. "Do I want to know what's stopping you from being here in the moment with me and turning you red while my cock is in you?"

"Probably not." I answer honestly.

He inches forward a bit more and I feel him at my hymen. A deep moan echoes in my throat at the feeling. "Tell me." He says. His mouth on my neck. Kissing. Licking. Oh god.

"I was…I um….I wondered…" He circles his hips. He doesn't inch deeper but the motion has him brush my clit with his body and I nearly explode from the sensation. Stars start to form in my eyes, then stop as he boops me on the nose again. I growl at him and all he does is chuckle and kiss me.

"Tell me."

I can't help but to blurt it out. "I was thinking about

porn." He freezes. His eyes wide, and brows high up on his forehead.

"You were thinking about porn? You watch porn?" He looks stunned. Almost like he doesn't know why I would even know what porn is.

"I've seen porn. I've masturbated." I say out loud. Then snap my mouth shut.

He groans and drops to his elbows, his forehead touching mine, but still keeping the bulk of his weight off of me. "Babe, why the fuck are you thinking about porn, when I'm trying to fuck you?"

"It's cause you looked down, so I looked down. I thought it looked hot, erotic, and then I wondered how many other people had the same thought. Then I thought, oh, a lot of people probably. Cause isn't that the point of porn." I rush the words out as quick as I can. I want this conversation done with. I want to get back to the sex.

"Fuck babe. Only you." He kisses me and rolls his hips. "I'm going to start moving again, you good with that?"

I nod and kiss his cheek. "Yes please."

He smiles and then his lips are on me. I lose myself to the kiss for a handful of seconds before my body erupts in agony. Holy shit! Massimo has thrust the rest of his impressive length and girth into me. Holy shit.

"I've got you babe. I know it hurt. It's almost over, then I can make you feel good. I promise." I nod. A single tear escaping my eye. I don't wipe it away, I let it fall down and get lost in my hairline. I breathe deeply a few times. The pain has subsided. I test it by rocking my hips up.

Massimo takes it as the invitation it was to move. He starts off slow pulling out a bit, then back in. Gradually taking more out each time until he has just the tip inside me, then slams home. The feeling is unlike anything I have ever felt before. I moan, I scream out his name.

"Liv. Fuck Liv. You feel so good. So fucking good. Never going to get enough."

I kiss him. I can't make sentences or even words more than his name and "oh god" come out of my mouth. Best I can manage is to dig my nails into his back, his forearms, his ass, and anything else I can reach. Then I kiss him until I feel the coil in me tighten. It's nearly painful my need to come. I hold off as best I can. I want him to come with me. I want this experience for the both of us.

"Babe, you close. I need you to be close."

"I'm close."

"Thank fuck." He murmurs as he leans his weight on one elbow and moves the other hand between us. I briefly wonder what he is doing until his finger brushes against my clit. Fuck me!

"Massimo!" I scream so loud as my body detonates into a symphony of fireworks. My muscles tense, my body trembles, my mind blanks, and nothing has ever felt this good. Nothing ever will.

As I float back to Earth, I feel more of Massimo's weight on me. I encourage it by putting a hand on the back of his neck and stroking his hair. His warm cum is flooding my insides. Mixing with my own. I wonder if I should be panicking. I'm not on birth control. And now I'm realizing he didn't wear a condom. Not that I would know the difference, but now I know I never want him to. I don't ever want anything between us.

CHAPTER SIXTEEN

Massimo

A week has gone by since I defiled my virgin.

I won't say those words to her or anyone else. They are all for me. Not only did I make love to her. I fucked her, hard. I took her on the bed, in the shower, against the window, and on the floor. Then when she was too tired to move, I ate her out like a man lost in the woods for a week.

I've gotten to have a repeat performance every day except for the next day. She literally held a knife between us and hand over her pussy when she threatened me. Told me she was too sore to take me again. Her threat had only made my cock want her more. I wasn't going to press. I was happy to give her the day. Or two if she needed. So I drew her a bath to help her relax and soothe the ache I gave her.

Only when I got her in there, and she felt my cock on her back again, she wouldn't stop touching it. I told her to ignore him. He had a mind of his own when it came to her. Well, so did she. She ended up giving me the best blow job of my life.

I swear I passed out for a moment. She looked so sexy when she was done. She tried to swallow. My load was too big. It ended up dripping out of her mouth.

Fuck me. I'm getting hard at the memory. Now isn't the time. We have work to do.

We are meeting with Ivan and his men today. He has his plan in place, the detail and strategies worked out. Our team will be backup to the Detroit Russians coming into the city. It's another reason we are in the meeting. Ivan wanted open communication with us. Reassuring that the extra men were not to wage war on us.

We are meeting in a back room of a restaurant Ivan owns. There are twenty of us in the room. Three Italians. Me, Luca, and Val. We brought our own teams with us as backup in case we ran into any trouble, or someone at the meeting tried to double cross Ivan. They are stationed in the restaurant, in our SUVs out back, and down the road in a little cafe.

Four hours later, we shake hands with Ivan, Viktor and the rest of the men. We have their plan in place, as well as our tentative plan for destruction of the Cartel. It's just a waiting game at this point.

Our car ride home follows our typical strategy. Me, Luca, and Val each in separate cars with our own bodyguards and soldiers. We don't take a direct path home, and we don't follow each other directly. A second car of soldiers follows each of us at a distance.

Ten minutes down the road, I get a call that stalls my heart. It's Luca, he's taking fire. Him and his men are ambushed. "Get to Luca." I yell to the driver.

We're two minutes out and it's the longest two minutes of my life.

I can't do anything but listen to the shots ringing from Luca's end of the call. He either dropped his phone, or forgot about us to fire back. Either way, I try to find the positive in the sound. The continued gunfire means that our team is still alive, still fighting, which means there is a good chance my best friend, my Don, my brother is alive.

We round the corner and see the fight. A few of our men are lying on the ground. I already know they are dead. They will be honored for their sacrifice. Sal, my driver, hits the gas instead of the breaks. I see why. There are a few of their men standing in the middle of the road, still firing, and making their way over to where I see Luca and Al crouched behind their overturned SUV.

There is a loud thud followed by the SUV lifting into the air for a moment as Sal mows the enemy down. The gunfire stops. The enemy is dead. I should be happy. I am happy. I am also mad I didn't get to shoot any of the bastards myself.

Luca and Al rush to the car. Luca barking orders to our support car as he does. He's ordering them to collect our men and check the bodies of the others. Luca whips the door open and he and Al scurry in. "Have you heard from Val?" He asks. There is panic in his voice.

"No, have you?" I had thought of him earlier, but I'll admit I was more worried about getting to my Don. It is what men in our family are trained to do.

"No. He's not answering his fucking phone." Growls Luca.

Al's got his phone out. "I'm pulling up his tracker now." He says. "Fuck. His sensor's not moving."

He should be moving. If things had gone according to plan, he would be at the Compound already. "Where is he?" I bark.

Al rattles off the location. It takes us four minutes to get there. The anger, fear, sadness, all sorts of emotions are rolling off of Luca. Val isn't just his Consigliere, his adviser, he is his brother. His blood brother.

We pull up to the location and Luca goes white. Val's pieces of the car are scattered along a hundred foot stretch of the road. The car itself is resting on its roof in the ditch. Bullet holes punched every few inches into the doors. "No, no, no." Shouts Luca as he practically dives over me and out the car. I run after him. My gun loaded and ready to take out any fucker that dare attack us again.

Luca bends down. A small sigh of relief hits him. "He's not here."

My head snaps to him, then I too duck down and look into the car. He's right. He's not. There is some blood, but it's not enough to be life threatening. "He's alive." I say.

"They took him." Says Luca. His gaze hard as steal. No one fucks with his family. And you sure as fuck don't fuck with his brother.

I know Luca. Shits about to get very dangerous in the streets of Chicago.

CHAPTER SEVENTEEN
Livianna

The Compound is in lock down and all hell has broken loose.

It's chaos. I want to help. I don't know where to go. Where to be. What to do. I want to ask Massimo what he needs. I won't though.

He stormed into the office with Luca an hour ago, only stopping for a brief moment to tell me we were on lock down and that he needed to go. Then he kissed my forehead and stomped after Luca. Then there was a lot of yelling. Some crashing and breaking of objects. Then I saw Ricco and Bosco running down the hall and going into the office. Guards rushed to various positions in the house. It's like everyone knew what to do, where to be, where to help, except me. I hadn't felt so alone or so much like an outsider since I sat in the basement. Even Elena rushed past me and into the office without a second glance.

I suppose her involvement does make sense though. She's a wizard with the computer. Massimo told me stories of everything she has hacked and the information she gathered that led to Santo being taken out and the rats in the family being rounded up. It was why my father had so many jobs I needed to help with before I was kidnapped. They had received an abundance of evidence and needed to force the rats out without making a scene.

The ones I worked with from other families like the Irish and Russian were their points of contact. I had a hunch that was the deal, I just didn't know Elena was at the source of it.

Milan finally takes pity on me standing awkwardly against the wall in the hall and brings me to the kitchen. She says she's witnessed a lock down a few times in her life. Each time she didn't know what do to help, and rather than be in the way, she went to the kitchen and cooked. "Even in the midst of chaos the men have to eat." She said.

So I here I am. Making sandwiches and coffee on repeat. Every time a tray is empty I make more. Each time the carafe of coffee is empty I brew more. I can see why Milan comes here during times like this. I may not be helping win whatever war is being waged out there, but in here I can help in my own small way.

Shortly after Milan and I started on sandwiches, Greta and Violet joined us. They set about making cookies and all variety of deserts.

"Sugar can be just as good as caffeine in these stressful moments." Comments Greta. She's right. A smile ticks at the corner of my mouth. I want to smile. Now isn't the time.

"Here sweetie, can you take this tray to our men?" Asks Greta. Her hands outstretched with a tray loaded with a selection of food and a pitcher of hot coffee and a stack of disposable cups. Our men meaning Massimo, Ricco and Bosco.

"Are you sure they won't mind me interrupting?" I question. I don't want them getting mad at me. I don't want to interrupt them and cause a delay in whatever it is that they are handling.

"Trust me. Massimo needs to see you. And everyone else will appreciate you thinking about them."

"Okay." I whisper. I'm not confident in this course of action. But to a degree, what she says makes sense.

I carry the tray down the hall. It's slightly heavy, but I make it to the door. Al is standing guard outside it. He smiles at me and takes a half of a turkey sandwich. "Thanks darling." He then turns to grab the door handle. With a knock he opens the door and says "they'll appreciate the spread." I smile at him and move inside the door.

Everyone in the room stops talking and stares at me. "Sorry." I hurry over to a side table and set the tray down. I go to turn to leave, but I'm stopped by a large set of arms picking me up. It's Massimo. His arms squeeze me almost to the point of pain. I don't whimper or say a word. Greta was right. Massimo needed me.

I hug him back. My legs going around his hips so he can put his hands under my butt to support me. He walks me back to the couch, were he falls down into its soft cushions. He tucks his head into the curve of my neck and shoulder and breathes me in. The tickle of his warm breathe sooths me.

I slowly stroke the hair at the base of his neck. He loves when I do it after sex, or whenever he is cuddling me.

"Massimo." Says Bosco. He's standing near a large round table, looking at us. Everyone is. No, not us. Me. Why are they looking at me?

"No." Replies Massimo, a bit louder and harsher than I expected.

"It's a good plan." Pipes in Elena.

I can't help but wonder what they are talking about. I won't ask. They can tell me if they want. Massimo's arms go tighter on me. He pulls my head down to his shoulder. I rest my cheek against him. It feels important that I stay in his arms. Just like this for the time being. "Not happening. I won't risk her."

Her?

Me.

They are talking about me. I try to pull away to look at Massimo. He won't let me. "I'm not risking you. It's not happening. Find another way." His voice cracks. My big scary Mafia man is scared. What is the plan? How bad could it be?

"We're running out of time." Whines Luca. He sounds distressed.

Massimo still won't let me move. So I don't. But I do start asking questions. "Time for what?"

Ricco is the one who answers. He comes closer to me. Moves so he is in my line of vision without me moving. "Val was kidnapped."

"What?" I screech. I try to extract myself again, but Massimo won't let me move an inch. "How, when?"

"A few hours ago. Two of our three convoys were attacked after the meeting with the Russians. Massimo's team got to Luca's in time to help. There wasn't enough time to get to Val before he was gone." Replies Ricco. I can see the pain of the unknown status and health of his son is taking a toll on his heart and soul. I wonder if Greta knows. She can't, can she? If she did, how could she have been so calm?

"How could I…" I try to say help. I don't get it out. Massimo stands abruptly and makes to walk to the door with me still in his arms.

"No." He grumbles over and over again. One word with each step he takes.

"Massimo." I say. "Massimo! MASSIMO!!" I try getting

louder each time before finally I settle for screaming and pulling his ear. He finally stops walking and loosens his hold enough so I can look him in the eye. "Massimo, listen to me. Can you do that?"

He nods.

"Good. Val is important, not just to Luca and Ricco, or the family. He is important to you. He is every bit your brother as Luca is. Right?" He nods again. "Is what they say true? Could I help bring him home?"

He starts to shake his head no.

"Mass. Honey. Focus. Can. I. Help. Him?" I over enunciate each word while maintaining eye contact.

He nods. It's barely there, but I see it. He doesn't want to admit it, but he doesn't want to lie to me.

"Then let me help." He starts to grumble and tighten his hold on me. "Massimo. Stop. This is what we signed up for. This is what it is to be a Caruso. We protect each other. So while me doing whatever it is you need me to do, I won't be doing it alone. Right now Val is alone. I know he's tough. I know he's a survivor. But truth of the matter is. He is alone. We need to get him out."

Massimo seems to finally concede. He kisses my forehead and lowers me to the ground. He takes my hand and walks me back to the table where everyone else is seated.

Luca reaches out for my hand. I take it and squeeze and don't let go. Massimo moves behind me. Putting his front to my back and holding me close.

"What's the plan?" I ask.

CHAPTER EIGHTEEN

Livianna

Things go mostly according to plan.

It feels like when I was doing jobs with dad. I'm dressed to impress and at a bar in the Russian neighborhood. Ivan knows I'm here. He's got a few men posted nearby. He can't put too many men on me, much to Massimo's frustration.

There are no Italians or Caruso men in the building, or out front. Again, much to Massimo's frustration.

I'm a golden egg. At least, that's what Bosco called me when they told me the plan. They had been tracking Joseph. The man that escaped me at the bar the day I was kidnapped. Online chatter that Elena discovered, revealed that Joseph knew the location of Val, and that he was meeting friends at this bar tonight.

My role as the golden egg is to catch the attention of Joseph. Get him to come to me so I can get him talking. There is a chance he knows who I am, and knows I'm with the Caruso's. If that is true, which is what Massimo fears. I will likely be drugged and kidnapped, then taken to a secondary location.

Everyone is aware of this plan and everyone signed off on it, including me.

Massimo is pissed at me. For good reason. I would be just as pissed if he was in my position and I his. Still, I volunteered for this, and I will take his wrath when I get home.

Home. God that feels good to say and have it refer to Massimo's place and not my tiny apartment. Which, I really should go back to someday. Massimo's been buying me clothes and whatever essentials I need. I honestly don't need much if anything from the apartment. I want to go back to clear it out. To close out that chapter of my life and show Massimo how much I'm devoted to him.

As for the plan. Joseph is making his way over to me now. My nerves tingle with anticipation. Good or bad, I am committed to this plan. Whatever happens, I know Massimo will come for me. I have an army at my back. They are only a minute out. I've got multiple trackers on me. One in my shoes. One in my necklace. One in my earring. And one implanted in my armpit. It's a weird location. But it made sense to put it there. Arms, backs, and even necks are all common places for them.

Hands and feet aren't practical, and are said to be quite painful locations for them. If I am grabbed, I may be stripped of my clothes, and jewels, or just one of the two. Then someone will search me for signs of a tracker. When they do that, I would be standing with my legs apart and my arms either to my sides or straight out. In that position, the armpit still has some shadows and hidden skin.

Also, who the hell would think to look in an armpit for a needle mark? Not me. Well, not me before this. Now, if I ever capture someone, I'll be looking.

When the hell would I need to capture someone?

Never. Although, I may need to help Massimo someday.

Shit. Where's my boop? I need Massimo to boop me, I'm going down a rabbit hole.

I look around myself discretely, seeing if anyone is watching me. Nope. Joseph is getting closer but his eyes aren't on me yet. Here goes.

"Boop." I whisper to myself as I touch my finger to my nose like Massimo.

Holy shit it worked. With my focus back, I force myself to appear casual. I order a drink from the bartender. A martini. I order it dirty. Not because I know what that means. It's because it sounds sexual. It's a proven technique that I found while working with dad.

"Hey gorgeous." Ugh that voice makes my skin crawl. It's Joseph.

I turn and slap on my best smile. "Hey handsome."

"What's a girl like you, doing all alone on a Friday night?" He asks. His eyes roving over my body. He licks his lips. Gross. Not happening.

I play my part like I've done so many times before. "I won't be alone long. My friend is coming. She's running late."

"Sorry to hear. I can keep you company while you wait. If you want?" He offers while gesturing to the empty seat next to me.

I nod and take a sip of my drink while he sits. His eyes stay focused on my mouth. Bingo. He's hooked.

Suddenly a loud commotion by the door starts. Four, no five, six, men are throwing punches. I turn quickly to look. The fight is getting bigger by the moment. I hop off my stool so as to not get knocked off it. I fall right into Joseph's waiting arms. Shit. I feel the cold press of metal against my back.

Not again.

"Here's how this is going to work babe. You're going to walk, calmly with me to the kitchens. You won't make a peep will you?"

I shake my head. Nope. No I won't. This wasn't the direction of the plan I was hoping for. But it is one we anticipated could be a possibility. Both the Caruso's and Ivan's teams are ready for this situation.

Or so I thought.

I get into the kitchen. Joseph immediately steps back and tells me to take off all my jewelry.

I do.

Then he tells me to take off the shoes and dress. Fuck. I hate this fucker. I want to kill him. I could disarm him. I know how. I did it with Massimo the night I was taken. But I can't. That's not the plan. We need to save Val. To do that, I need this twat to take me to him.

Once I'm stripped, he throws his oversized coat at me. He doesn't have to tell me to put it on. I do it as soon as it is in my hands. Then he is leading me roughly by the arm into the walk-in refrigerator. What the hell? This can't be where Val is.

It's not. Along the back wall, Joseph moves a box of fries, then pushes against the wall. It opens up and reveals a stairwell. Shit.

We walk down the flight of steps, then what feels like a football field length hall. Then we are going up another set of stairs that opens into a storage closet of a closed antique's shop. By the layer of dust that is coating, well, everything, it looks like no one has used the store as a store in a long time. Years probably.

He leads me out the back door and to an awaiting car. I so hope Massimo or Elena, someone is actively watching my tracker. If anyone at the bar saw me head into the kitchen, they would have alerted the men outside that I could be going out the back. When I didn't would they immediately look for me, or think I'm wooing him into talking in the kitchen?

I don't have long to think before we are stopping and I am being ushered out of the car. Joseph has a tight grip on my arm as he drags me up the front steps of an old Victorian house. This too looks long abandoned. Except for the small gathering of soldier's that sit around a table playing cards, and the two we passed on the way in.

"We are not to be disturbed, understood?" Joseph announces to the room. The men just wave him off. That tells me a lot. It tells me he isn't the boss. He doesn't hold a high rank. And the men don't respect him. This could also mean they don't care about him. Good. I may need to use that information later.

I'm dragged up the stairs. Not because I fear what he is planning. I'm confident Massimo will be here before he touches me. No, I'm dragging my feet and purposely stumbling so I can have every second available to me to search the rooms we pass and go through for signs of Val.

He has to be here.

Bingo.

Upstairs and the second room on the right, I see him. He's strapped to a chair. He looks like shit. One of his eyes are swollen shut, his nose is bleeding and crooked, and he is slumped to the side. He is in severe pain. I wonder how bad his internal injuries are.

I want to yell to him. I want to tell him to not give up. Help is coming. We came for him.

But I can't. I can't alert Joseph to anything yet.

After we pass the room Val is in, Joseph pushes me into a

room across the hall. There is a mattress on the floor, and a lopsided dresser leaning against one wall. There is also a door to my right. It's open. Looks like it leads to a bathroom.

While Joseph turns his back to me to lock the door. He stuffs his gun into the back of his pants. Stupid move Joe.

I grab the gun and hall ass for the bathroom. I don't shoot him. The gunshot would be heard by the men downstairs. The cavalry isn't here yet. I don't know if they are seconds away or minutes. They are coming, that's all I am certain of. Which means my only job left is to stay alive.

Joseph is quicker than I thought he would be. And the door is flimsier than I had hoped. As the door comes crashing off its hinges and slams into the counter. It snaps further and the top half shatters the mirror, sending pieces of the glass scattering around the floor and sink.

I toss the gun into a bin of dirty towels. It vanishes from sight. Good. Hopefully Joseph won't find it. I can handle him hand to hand, but weapons make things more difficult.

He either doesn't see the gun, or doesn't care. He rushes to me with an audible roar. Our bodies collide and send us to the floor. I quickly roll and get behind him. I grab the shower curtain and yank it off its bar. I pull the fabric around his neck. I then wrap it several times around both my hands so I have a good grip. Then I pull back. Hard. I keep pulling, all while he struggles. Slowly his arms lose strength. His breathing slows. Then his movements stop.

I'm not sure if he is passed out or dead. I don't take the time to find out, I scramble to my feet and make to run. I don't get far before a hand wraps around my ankle. My forward momentum is stopped, which send my body crashing to the floor.

Joseph climbs on top of me. His body pinning me to the floor. My hands are free so I punch and scratch every piece of

144

his face I can. He howls in pain. Then he punches me in the face. My head snaps to the side.

Shit. That hurt. My vision blurs for a moment. When it clears. I feel his hands around my neck. Choking me like I just choked him.

A shimmer of something shiny catches my attention. Glass. The mirror. I reach out as far as I can to reach it. My fingertips graze it but I can't yet get a grip. I try again. The edges of it slice painfully into my fingers. I can't worry about that. I'm slowly losing the ability to breath. My lungs burn from the lack of oxygen. Finally I feel my fingers catch it and drag it closer to me. I pick it up, the edge cutting into my palm. Don't care.

This is all I needed. This will buy me the time I need until Massimo gets here.

I hope.

CHAPTER NINETEEN

Massimo

I'm going out of my fucking mind waiting like this. What the fuck is Joseph waiting for? He's just sitting there talking to his buddies. It's been thirty minutes. Come on fucker. Look at the bar. Look at Liv. She's right there. My golden goddess is offering herself up on a silver fucking platter. Take it.

Take it so I can fucking end you.

A few more minutes pass, then finally, finally, Joseph makes his way to the bar. He makes a beeline straight for Livianna.

I hate that I'm not there. I hate that I'm two blocks away watching on Elena's tablet where she has hacked into the security cameras in the bar so that we can have eyes inside.

Suddenly a fight breaks out in the bar. Starts with four men. Quickly escalated to ten. They are knocking over tables and chairs. I lose sight of Liv in the commotion. Then the camera's cut out.

"What the fuck?" I growl.

Elena reaches for the tablet. I had been holding it.

Refusing to let it go while we watched. Everyone else was looking over my shoulder at the screen from inside our van. "Give me." Says Elena as it's ripped out of my hands. Luca is immediately dialing on his phone. Calling Ivan no doubt. His men are in the bar. We aren't completely blind. They will watch over Liv for us.

"What do you mean she's gone?" Shouts Luca.

I rip the phone from his ear and put it on speaker. "So help me god Ivan, if anything happens to my woman..." I let the threat linger in the air. I don't give a fuck what Mafia he belongs to or what alliance they have agreed on. If my woman is hurt I will fucking burn the world to the ground.

"Relax Massimo. This is what you wanted. You wanted him to take her and lead you to Val. This is how he is going to do it. Get your heart out of your ass, pull up your tracker app and tell me where the fuck my men are going."

A snarky retort is on my lips, but I bite it back. He's right. We have the trackers.

Nope. The app pulls up. Had the trackers. Four still show in the bar, and the fifth, the fucking armpit one, is still in her. It's moving fast. Looks like she's in a car.

I start barking directions to both Al, our driver, and Ivan on the phone. He's closer by a few minutes. "Promise me Ivan. Promise me you will get to her as quickly as you can."

"I promise. You can thank me later by helping me take down Mishkin."

A smile spreads on my face. I can't wait to make that fucker pay. He may never have gone to war with us, but he fucked with a lot of innocent women and children in Chicago. His reign will come to a bloody end soon. "Abso-fucking-lutely." I reply.

"I'm pulling up on the building. We're going in." Then he's gone. The fucker hung up on me. I throw the phone at the wall of the van. It shatters the screen and clatters to the floor.

"Was that necessary?" Asks Elena.

Her head is still down. Still typing away. She won't stop. Not until we find Val, Liv, and take down Ramirez. Even then, she might not. She likes to stay busy, and there is never a shortage of enemies when you rule an Empire.

Before Al can put the van in park, I am leaping out of the door, I don't hear anymore gunfire. I want to take that as a good thing. Liv isn't outside. She's not standing here waiting for me.

Fuck no!

My gun is out and ready to fire, just in case some shady fuck tries to get the drop on one of us when we let our guard down. I feel like I'm running in circles. Going room by room I don't see her. I don't see Val. "Where the fuck is she?" I roar.

"Mass." I hear Luca call for me. He's standing at the bottom of a staircase that I somehow missed.

I rush back to it, hoping to find her on the stairs. She's not. I run up the stairs two at a time. Luca is right behind me. My head whips side to side as I scan the rooms as I pass them. Two doors down we find Val. Luca and I rush to him. He's bleeding, bruised, and probably has a few broken bones, but he's alive, and he's breathing. Luca shouts for Elena to call the doctor.

I get up and scan the room she's not here. "Liv's not here." I turn to Luca. He's cutting through the bindings around Val's feet. "This is your fault. I told you I couldn't risk her."

Luca looks grief stricken as he stares back at me. "If there had been any other way to end this, I would have. You know I would have. She's not here. It doesn't mean she's dead. Just like with Val. They took her alive."

"Massimo?" Calls a voice from the hallway. It's not my Liv. But maybe they found her.

What if he hurt her? What if he....he…

I can't finish that thought. I can't imagine my beautiful girl getting sexually assaulted. We'll deal with whatever happens. It doesn't matter what. We are strongest together. I'll get her through whatever nightmare she survived. I just need her.

We'll get through this. She won't be leaving my side for a long time. If ever. And she damn well won't be leaving the compound.

Rushing out of the room, I'm directed by a Russian soldier to go right. Another Russian stands at a door a little ways down and across the hall. I recognize him. He's Ivan's second. As I reach him, he side steps to allow me to pass him and enter the room. He doesn't speak. His face set in firm line. Neither telling me good, nor bad news. Fuck why can't I read people like Liv. She could give him one glance and tell me what he was thinking.

Inside the room, I find Ivan standing in the entry of what appears to be a bathroom. Moving closer, my heart pounds painfully in my chest. There is a puddle of blood on the floor in the bathroom. Just beyond Ivan's feet.

Oh god.

Please don't let that be Livianna's.

Please don't let that be my girl's.

Ivan turns and smiles. He fucking smiles. Instantly my heart soars. She's alive. I don't see her yet, but I know.

"You need to teach your woman to turn off the safety." He says as he shifts out of the doorway and gives me room to enter. "She's been pulling the trigger of the gun for a solid minute at me." He says.

I pay no attention to his words. All I can see, all I care

about is my girl. My sweetheart. She's crouched between the toilet and the shower stall. She's bloody and disheveled.

She's alive.

And she's practically fucking naked.

The distinctive click of the trigger being pulled with no boom of a bullet has my heart pounding. Ivan wasn't lying. She's pulling the trigger. Is she pulling it at me? What the fuck happened? I'm whipping my shirt off over my head so I can put it on her before I take her away from this place.

Getting closer I can see her eyes aren't looking at me. They are looking past me, to the corner. I follow her gaze and find Joseph's body. His chest looks like it was mauled by a bear. A piece of what looks like mirror, is sticking out dead center.

The air is knocked from my lungs. She killed him. It's the second fucking time my girl has had to kill to survive. Never again. She won't need to spill anymore blood. That's my fucking job.

I move in front of her. I keep back a foot until her focus comes back. "Liv." I whisper. I don't want to scare her too bad when she's in a trance like this. "Sweetheart." I say a little louder, and reach out my hand to boop her nose.

It works. It fucking works like a charm every time.

"Mass!" She screams. Then she drops the gun and scrambles to get out of her corner and into my arms. I catch her body mid-air and bring her close. Our lips find each other in a heated kiss.

I pull away after too brief a time. My hands run all over her body. Checking for injuries and where the fuck all the blood is coming from. "It's not mine." She says.

I don't believe her. My hands keep moving until I get to her hands. She has a deep gash on her right hand. I hold her hand up to prove my point. She sighs, then leans in for me to hold her close again. "Okay, so it's not all my blood. I promise. That's the only spot. The mirror cut me when I stabbed him with it.

"Blood thirsty little thing." Ivan says with a laugh from the door. "Stole my kill. He killed my cousin. Though, I suppose your girl did a good job making it painful. Fucker was choking on his own blood when I came in."

Livianna wrenches herself from Massimo's arms and vomits all over Joseph's body. Causing Ivan to laugh.

"Just when I didn't think I could like you Italians more!" He continues to laugh as he leaves the room. "I hope my future wife is just like this one."

"Mine." I growl.

"Yours." Livianna agrees as she presses her forehead to mine.

CHAPTER TWENTY

Livianna

It's been a few weeks. Things are relatively calm around here. Val is healing nicely. Though he hasn't woken up yet. The surgeon is still here. Luca refuses to let her leave. She's not our usual Doctor. She's a surgeon. She was called in to save Val when they couldn't get him to the hospital. The Compound was closer, and he was bleeding out.

She's a beast in the infirmary. Doesn't take shit from any of the men. It's amazing to watch. I've gotten to spend a bit of time with her the last few days. Partially cause I feel bad for her. I know what it's like to be kidnapped and kept in this place. The other reason is because I'm late. It's only a few days, but mine are always on time.

She handed me a stick to pee on a few minutes ago. She offered me the bathroom in the infirmary to take it. I declined. I needed to be alone while I panic. So here, I am. Hiding in the bathroom of one of the many guest rooms waiting for the timer on my phone to go off.

Three minutes. Feels like more. I'm not sure what I'm

hoping the test will say. I feel like I already know. My breasts are already tender and I've been getting nauseous at random times of the day. It started a week ago. I thought it was delayed stress or panic from everything that happened.

I have nightmares sometimes and the scar on my hand is a reminder of my second kill.

I don't feel bad. He deserved it. Even without considering what he did to me. His death is justified after all the women's lives he's ruined.

Still, as I sit here, I wonder if I can do this. Am I cut out to be a mother? Is this life any place for a child? If it is a boy, how much blood will be on his hands? If a girl, will she end up like me? Will she get into dangerous situations and need to spill blood? Will she be targeted, attacked?

Panic is threatening to consume me. I barely notice the door being opened. I look up just as Massimo is pocketing his tools. Damn man hates when I lock the door between us. He removed our bathroom door handle after the last time I did it.

I just wanted to use the bathroom in peace. Without him hovering. His protective instincts since the events have been overwhelming. Most times I love it. I feel safe with him around. He keeps both the nightmares at night and the dark thoughts during the day away.

My therapist says it's normal after what I've been through. Funny. I didn't think the Mafia men had therapists. Boy was I wrong. There are several.

All trusted members of the family. I wonder how bad their nightmares are? I imagine they have them after the horrible stories they must hear.

"Swear to god woman, I will handcuff you to the bed if you make me hunt you down again." I smile. I can't help but to smile around him. He is the light of my life.

My smile must not reach my eyes because he rushes to

me. "What's wrong? Are you sick?"

My eyes flick to the test on the counter as my phone alarm sounds. It's time to look.

"Is that?" He asks, nodding to the test.

I don't have words so I nod back.

"Are you?" I shrug. "You haven't looked?"

"Not yet." I reply.

"Are you scared?

I think for a moment and answer honestly. "No. Are you?" I don't let him answer yet. I see his mouth open and panic. "I know we didn't plan this. We haven't been together long. We haven't talked about..."

He stops me with a kiss. "I love you. We might not have planned it, and we definitely didn't try to prevent it." He says with a wink. "But I'm not scared. I love you. I want everything with you. Marriage, babies, fights, make-up sex, a house, a dog...."

"Of course you would include sex."

"With you? Always!" I laugh and he brings his forehead to mine. "Are you ready to know?"

I nod my head. Then ask the question I've asked myself. "Will you be disappointed I'm not?"

"Fuck no." His reaction gives me pause. But then he continues and it warms my heart. "Just means I get to keep trying to knock you up."

I laugh. "So you're saying if I am, we won't be having more sex?"

"Absolutely not. We'll be having celebratory sex."

"And that's different how?" I ask.

"It'll be on the bed." He replies with a massive grin.

"And if we aren't? Where will it be?"

He doesn't hesitate to answer. "Floor, against the wall, on the couch, in the kitchen, hood of my car..." He says each one with a kiss down my neck.

"Best find out what the test says before you make too many plans." I tease.

"Too late." He says with a smirk as he grabs the test and flips it over. "Bed it is."

About Nova Mason

Nova Mason made her debut with her first novel "Running: Caruso Mafia Book One". The series continued with Massimo's story in "Hunting" and will continue with Val's in "Fighting". She fell in love with books while still in the womb and learned to read at only three. Her goal as a kid was to read every book in the children's section of the local library one shelf at a time. Sadly they remodeled before she could complete her goal. Now she's working to fill the library in her house with books she loves and a shelf or two dedicated to her own stories.

She loves hearing from her readers, so please don't hesitate to drop her a note on one of her social media sites.

Printed in Great Britain
by Amazon